A Spirit Rises

STORIES BY

Sylvia Townsend Warner

THE VIKING PRESS   *New York*

*Published in 1962 by The Viking Press, Inc. .
625 Madison Avenue, New York 22, N. Y.*

All the stories in this collection, except for "Randolph" and
"The Snow Guest," appeared originally in *The New Yorker*.

Library of Congress catalogue card number: 62-11675

Printed in the U.S.A. by The Murray Printing Company

Second printing April 1962

To
William Maxwell

My thanks are due to
The New Yorker in
which many of these stories
originally appeared.

Contents

YOUTH AND THE LADY

———

He was lying face downward on the turf. The sun was hot on his back, but the uncultivated ground still retained the coldness and damp of winter. He had lain there for so long that his body's warmth had overcome the cold in the ground, but he was still conscious of the damp. The sensation was relaxing, and vaguely congenial, as though he were lying in a puddle of his own blood. He was lying on the brow of a hillside, where the ground curved sharply enough to exert a compulsion on him to slide gradually forward. His attitude countered the compulsion. He was looking through a pair of field glasses; his elbows, taking his forward weight, both propped and braked him, while his narrow feet in heavy brogue shoes trailed out behind him like a couple of anchors. He was in considerable discomfort and rapturously happy. His age was seventeen, his name was Martin Jones, and the Easter holiday had brought him back to his home in mid-Wales.

Larks were singing overhead. An occasional spurt of sound came from the road, whose curving ascent of the ridge brought it within a quarter of a mile of where he lay and then swung it to the north-west. It was mostly holiday traffic, private cars speeding over this undistinguished stretch of pastoral country to get to the mountains and eat sandwiches there. The ground in front of him fell away into a wooded valley. It was natural woodland, scrubby and overcrowded, with a dense undergrowth of hazels and honeysuckle. Here and there a tall tree stood up from it, and looked gaunt and unaccomplished, being slower to put on its foliage than the trees below. It was on one of these tall trees that the field glasses were trained.

The kites were building.

The kite, *Milvus milvus*, is a native British bird. Its narrow wings have a span of over five feet, its flight is powerful and adroit. It is a scavenger, taking its prey on the ground, and in the past it was as much a town bird as the sparrow is, feeding on rats, offal, and carrion. It is now so exceedingly rare that naturalists who see a kite are scrupulous not to endanger its existence by saying so.

During the previous summer holidays, Martin was walking through the woods with a friend when a clatter and a swish of wings caused them to look up. A long rufous tail, noticeably forked, vanished behind a sycamore. 'Good Lord,' said the friend, 'what an enormous bird! I believe it must be a kite.' Martin with cool presence of mind replied, 'My good idiot, don't you know a buzzard when you see one? If you could refrain from making your usual row, and listen for a moment, we'd probably hear it mewing.' Though he felt ready to faint, he had remembered that kites, like buzzards, mew.

After Harrison had left he went back several times, looking and listening. The kite had not appeared again. It was probably on its way somewhere else. The Christmas holiday was a washout; he had to go to Paris with an aunt. But on Palm Sunday, his first day at home, going to the brow of the hill for another look, he had seen a pair of kites circling overhead. They vanished downwind, they reappeared. They plunged into the wood. They were building! He was quite sure they were building when, scouting along the edge of the wood, he saw a tramp's toe-rag. No tramp would dress his toes in a place so full of thistles. Kites will twine bits of rag into their nests.

The problem now arose how to protect them. They were already endangered enough by their own recklessness. Spring had gone to their heads, they flew about mewing and making spectacles of themselves with no more prudence than the larks and a great deal more conspicuously. Three or four pair of kites, perhaps, in the whole of England were extant and nesting; and here were these two showing off like a circus. But Nature, if you come to think of it, makes no admission of rarity. A flower, the last of its species, will scatter its seeds over the concrete base of a cattle trough, and the few kites who have escaped the poultry farmer, the gamekeeper, and the collector build their nests in tall trees where any fool can see them, where any exterminating bird fancier can climb up to steal the eggs. Martin's parents took it for granted that he would be away all day, or alternatively all night—for badgers, too, are worth attention; the kites were safe enough as far as his father and mother were concerned. But how was he to cover up the fact that he was now going day after day to the same spot? He was not the only observer in the sparsely populated landscape. The postman, cycling along the track to Upper Llancaer to deliver Mr. Pritchard's *Daily Herald*; the driver of the milk lorry; Mrs. Gwennie Thomas, for ever darting out to see what her ducks were doing; and other, unidentifiable hazards—some distant human dot laying a hedge or trimming a copse—would soon notice his regular comings and goings, and remark in the course of conversation at The Lamb Inn, 'Young Jones the Rectory is walking up the road every morning. Funny, isn't it?' So every day he had to vary his route,

setting out in a contrary direction and then taking a cir-
cumbendibus, or ostentatiously dawdling along by the
brook as though he nursed some foul design on Gwennie's
old drake, or skulking behind stone walls, or lurking in
thickets, and once asking a lift in the milk lorry as far as
the old chapel and then making his way back along the
valley—all of which entailed many needless miles and
wasted a great deal of his precious time.

To-day he had been artful enough to revert to the road
and the direct route to his observation post on the brow,
whence he could look down over the wood and watch the
growth of the nest. Before long, the leaves would unfurl
and hide it, and this, though frustrating, would be a weight
off his mind. They were a capricious pair, his kites.
Throughout yesterday, the sky had been empty of them,
and he had trudged home in fury and despair, thinking that
some fool letting off a gun, some yelling girlish band of
primrose-gatherers, had caused them to desert. But to-day
they were back and, in their desultory artistic way,
busy.

All at once, they both flew up and hovered. They had
seen something. He detached his sight from the world of
the field glasses and looked behind him. A woman was
approaching; she was half-way between him and a large
shiny car, drawn up and vacated at the side of the road.
With a rapid movement, he thrust the field glasses between
his belly and the ground—not a sensible move, really, but
it must have been some obscure protective instinct, such as
teaches the hen bird to gather her chicks underwing. Then
he yawned, and stretched his arms. Then he lit a cigarette.
That, surely, looked very natural. Wriggling on his belly,
which made the field glasses even more insistent, he turned

a little to one side, so that out of the corner of his eye he could keep a watch on her. She was middle-aged, and not local. Habitat: not established. Plumage: expensive. Gait: tripping—for she walked on high heels. She was quite certainly walking towards him. Well, what of it? She might have lost her way, she might have got a puncture. Now she stopped short, and appeared to be in some sort of trance. Now, catching his eye, she smiled and came towards him with more decision. Perhaps she was a sex maniac.

'Excuse me,' she began (Habitat: the U.S.A.). 'Excuse me, but can you tell me what those birds are?'

Staring her in the face, he replied, 'Buzzards.'

'Buzzards?' Her voice was resolutely incredulous. 'Did you say they are buzzards?'

'Buzzards,' he repeated.

'Well, you surprise me. We've got buzzards at home. They're large birds, and I've never heard them sing.'

'Oh! You mean the larks?'

He felt his whole being change with the ecstasy of his relief. As though her face were a mirror to his feelings, he saw it relax, soften, flush with pleasure, with emotion, with a profound piety of acceptance.

'They're larks,' she said, hushing her voice.

She was a tall woman, but she seemed to grow taller as she stood and listened.

'There's one going up,' he said. 'Look!'

She watched the lark ascending, following it with her gaze. Her watching melted into listening. She stared and heard. Then, as though suddenly recalling his existence, she said, 'Well, thank you very much. All my life, I've wanted to hear the skylark.'

She walked slowly away. After going a little distance, she paused, and presently she paused again. Even when she had got into her car, she waited for several minutes before she started the engine and drove on.

THE LOCUM TENENS

BECAUSE of the telephone, Dr. Adam Hutton, the newly arrived locum tenens, was occupying the conjugal bedroom. He got into bed, tilted the reading lamp, and pulled up the eiderdown. The moment he laid hold of it, he remembered the roast fowl at supper. The roast fowl had been good and substantial; so was the eiderdown, and the phrase 'spotlessly clean', which the eiderdown demanded as its due, could . have applied with equal propriety to the fowl's accompanying bread sauce.

Everything in the room brandished cleanliness, merit, and substantiality, while, at the same time, the colouring of wallpaper, carpet, and curtains plainly indicated that they had been chosen because they would not show dirt. 'All the best bedrooms in Horn Street must have been like this,' he said to himself. 'Still are, for that matter, I dare say.' Behind a chink in the curtains (he had pulled them apart to look out) the windowpane glittered like a diamond, and in through the opened window came the familiar, grimy smell of the industrial West Riding. He had not smelled it for nearly thirty years.

But in his youth he had only guessed at such bedrooms, deducing them from furniture shops and advertisements. The cleanliness, merit, and substantiality of his own surroundings had been of a shabbier, more arduous kind, and the smell of grime much more insistent, while he, with the thudding industry of a small engine, had fought to learn, and to be able to go on learning, until, by the end of his

17

teens, he had finally learned himself out of his station and away from his birthplace, never to return. Get-on-and-get-out, get-on-and-get-out, get-on-and-get-out . . . If they had not been the words of his private heart, the printing shop across the street would have dinned them into him.

And he was still within the letter of his vow. He had not returned. This was Mexley, not Goatbridge. Identical in griminess and clatter, eclectic hideousness of public buildings and stoical ugliness of working-class streets, Mexley and Goatbridge and Hudderbeck and Wendon and Gullaby, sprawling one into another and laced together by trolley buses, were identical in mutual contempt, Goatbridge averring that folk in Hudderbeck never shut a door after them, Hudderbeck and Wendon cherishing a legend of what went into Mexley pies, Mexley, Goatbridge, Wendon, and Hudderbeck jeering at Gullaby greenhorns, and Gullaby on its hillside looking down on their smoky rooftops as on the Cities on the Plain. 'God knows what got into my head,' said Adam Hutton; and opening the street map of Mexley, which was not Goatbridge, he began to memorize its layout. Knowing Goatbridge, he found it easy enough to put Mexley together by its street names. Foundry Street, Wharf Street, Hoggle Yard and Slaughter Yard and Tanhouse Yard, Bull Ring and Laystall Lane—that would be the old part of the town. And Douro Crescent and Portico Place would be the former residential quarter, left now to brass-plate users, solicitors, and town offices—so he need not trouble to memorize that square of the map. Odd, though, that he could not find Horn Street. Realizing that Horn Street had got in from Goatbridge and that he was half asleep, he put out the light.

In his dream it was a Christmas morning, and the Goatbridge Brass Band was standing on the roof of the fire station, playing 'Christians, awake! Salute the happy morn.' But he was in a double bed in Mexley, and the telephone was ringing. A voice that might have come from any one of his aunts said, 'Is that you, Doctor? I'm in the call box—Mrs. Bella Heaton—and it's Joseph. He's been throwing up these last three hours, and I don't like the look of his nose, and his feet are like ice, and——'

'I'll come at once. But first tell me your address.'

A voice completely changed and concealing ineffable astuteness remarked, 'You aren't Dr. Walker, though.'

'No. Dr. Walker's in Wales, on his holiday. I'm doing his work. Now, tell me where you live.'

'Oh! Well, I dare say you might as well as not.'

As he left his room a door across the landing opened, and Miss Linda Walker appeared. 'Oh dear! Your first night, too. I'm so sorry.' She wore a blue dressing gown. She had put on her spectacles. Her hair stood out like brass filings. 'Can you manage? Will you be able to find your way?'

'Perfectly. Mustn't wake your mother.'

*

When he returned the hall light was on, and a thermos, a mug, and a plate of sandwiches stood on the hall table. Yorkshire hospitality. Mrs. Bella Heaton had already forced cocoa and seedcake on him. But he ate the sandwiches, for the raw air had given him an appetite. After leaving his patient he had gone to view Goatbridge by the pale moonlight, driving back by the Gullaby Road, whence Gullaby Old Church, silhouetted on the hilltop, looked as alarming as ever, gaunt and yet glutted, its churchyard crammed with enormous, jostling black headstones.

Breakfast was at eight. Porridge, ham and eggs, pikelets, potted shrimps, a blazing fire at his back, and a purple radiance shed on Mrs. Walker's spotlessly white hair from the band of coloured glass in the window. He was so insistently fed that he could barely get in his thanks for the thermos and sandwiches.

'Linda's her father's daughter,' said Mrs. Walker in tones of mild pride. 'She knows. What's our motto in this house, Linda dear?'

'Keep up the doctor, and he'll keep up the patient.'

'That's right. And you may rest assured, Doctor, if you should be out on a night call, Linda will always have something ready for you, no matter how often. And when you've finished your breakfast, she will be ready to show you the files and the forms and the registers and the day-book and the appointment lists. Linda does all the book-work, and she's qualified as a dispenser. She'll make a wonderful wife for a doctor, one of these days.'

Even for a mother, Mrs. Walker was shameless. Linda was not shameless; she was merely willing.

Adam had no fears. It was only a fortnight, and he could be heartless for much longer than that. He would be heartless, civil, and inscrutable.

But as the day wore on, with surgery hours, and visiting, and midday dinner, and visiting, and a groaning tea table, and surgery hours again, it was to himself that he grew inscrutable. What the devil had possessed him to come here —what sentimental lunacy, what decrepitude of mind?

Getting on and getting out, he had finished his training, and travelled on a research scholarship, and passed the war years as an Army doctor, and spent his accumulated pay on buying a partnership in a South Coast practice; and then, not liking the shape of National Health Service, had got out of that and into the research laboratories of a new firm that was making a good thing out of vaccines and antibiotics. There he proposed to remain, well paid, well thought of, interested in what he was doing, and near enough to London to be able to ease himself into a degree of culture that would make his old age creditable and entertaining. And then, because he was glancing through the *British Medical Journal* in order to compare his firm's advertisement with the advertisements of other firms, 'Mexley, West Riding,' caught his eye. What followed was dementia. Reading that Dr. James Walker required a locum tenens during the second fortnight in March, and even while scornfully commiserating the wretch who could only get away for that meagre release, he became convinced that if he did not snatch at this chance of going to Mexley, the rest of his life would be meaningless. So intense was his madness that not even the words 'live as family' could deter him. He had been going to Rome in April. Changing the date of his holiday, he arranged to go to Mexley in March. But why? But why? To be within smelling distance of the Goatbridge gasworks when the wind blew from the sweet south? To hear the Mexley Choral Society rehearsing Stainer's *Crucifixion*? To discover experimentally what went into a Mexley pie?

With the whole vehemence of his Goatbridge breeding, he exclaimed, 'Mexley!'

*

But by his third day in Mexley, subdued by hard work and harsh air, grossly hungry, grossly sleepy, shamelessly trifling with Mrs. Walker's shamelessness, and automatically relying on Linda's willingness, Adam began to feel it almost a matter of course to be there. In the preliminary correspondence, Walker had said that he would leave a detailed list of the patients under treatment, so that his locum might know from the start what would be required of him. This list turned out to be a great many slips of waste paper scribbled over with mysterious abbreviations—patients and treatments intermingled with memoranda about drugs that would need to be replenished, lyings-in to be expected, and fishing tackle that Dr. Walker would want on his holiday. These were piously handed over by Linda, but every morning she supplemented them with a neatly written schedule, telling him in a sweet full voice that Mr. Bucklaw and Mrs. Protheroe were cancers, that Miss Eden's boy was an epileptic, Mr. Murgatroyd a faker.

'And old Mrs. Robertson—she'll expect to be looked in on to-day—is another. But you mustn't tell her so; otherwise she'll send for you in the middle of the night with a heart attack.'

'I don't know why your father wanted a locum. You could do it all, and cook the pudding into the bargain. Who are these other regulars for to-day?'

Smiling, flushed with pleasure, she replied, 'Mr. Holmes, disseminated sclerosis. Ben Trotter, Parkinson's disease. Miss Rawson, arthritic and bedridden. Mrs. Ackroyd, cardiac dropsy. They're all in Tanhouse Yard, so you'd better leave your car in Bull Ring. And if nobody answers the door at Number Eleven—that's Mrs. Ackroyd—it will be because the niece she lives with is out fitting. She dressmakes. So just walk in and up the stairs to the front bedroom. But mind the stairs. Father says they're rotten, and the coffin will have to come out by the window.

They're shocking places, those houses in Tanhouse Yard. They ought to be pulled down. Nobody lives there but remainders.'

Still flushed, still smiling, she straightened the papers and went away; for it was part of her willingness that she knew when she was done with. As soon as she was out of the room, he unstraightened them again, pencilling in queries and alternative medicaments. Walker was still in the epoch of *Ferri Phos.*, *Tinct. Val.*, and *Card. Co.* This was a pity; for as a musician reading a single orchestral part can deduce quite a lot about the composer's merits Adam, reading Walker's clinical notes, often perceived acumen, and sometimes even diagnostic brilliance. Someone really ought to overhaul the old man and bring him up to date.

Most of the younger patients were ready enough to be brought up to date. They had read articles on modern medicine in popular papers, knew that recent discoveries were wonderful, and asked if they couldn't have some of these injections, like Aunt Gertie when she died in the hospital. No such readiness was shown in the quarter between Foundry Street and Laystall Lane, where the uncontaminated voice of Mexley remarked, 'Doctor never give me blue physic' or 'Haven't you any of t'old stuff left?' or 'Never set eyes on nowt like this.'

Miss Rawson, arthritic and bedridden, whom he found standing on a stepladder in a long flannel nightdress, engaged in putting a bit of shine on the gas bracket, consulted him about her football pools and, finding that he didn't know much about them, gave him a long lecture on how to do permutations. When he got away, he almost flinched under the westering light, which had broken through the day's long dullness. Every detail of Tanhouse

Yard was as brilliantly affirmed as if Vermeer had painted it. There was no answer when he knocked on the door of No. 11, so he pushed it open, to be confronted by a dressmaker's dummy, alarmingly actual in a flimsy white satin wedding dress. If it had not been for Linda's directions, he might have taken it for the ghost of Anne Boleyn or some such headless heroine. But, of course, that onslaught of raw light had left him dazzled.

He went upstairs and into the front bedroom, and into another attack of light and of pictorial quality. The high double bed faced the window. Exactly centred in the bed was an elderly woman, sitting up against a heap of pillows. She must have been a fine robust creature in her time, and she still displayed tokens of an obstinate vitality; for her hair was the hair of a young woman—smooth nut-brown hair, very thick, and plaited into two great ropes that hung down over her subsided breasts. But what overwhelmed him was the way she queened it over the bed. Never—so it seemed to him—had he seen a bed so mastered, so possessed, by its occupant; and though she had those subject pillows heaped behind her, her spinal column needed no such support. Straight and sufficient, it could have carried the weight of a pediment poised on that large shapely head with its ropes of plaited hair.

'Mrs. Ackroyd?'

'Aye.'

Her voice conveyed nothing beyond local breeding and the fact that this was no Miss Rawson to delay him in conversation. He asked his questions and examined her. To judge by her disease, she might be dead in a couple of months; to judge by her physique, she might live another two years. Her answers were brief, plain, and dismissing, as though she knew all this for formality and waste of time. Her instinct tells her not to talk, he thought. A big black-and-white cat lay beside her, as unforthcoming as she. 'Company for you,' he said, constrained by her lack of conversation to say something, however flat.

'That's right.'

Her eyes were so sunk into the stained caverns of their sockets that he could not tell their colour, or the direction of their glance. She did not turn her head, but as he opened his case and stood debating whether his alternative to the medicine Dr. Walker had been giving her would be any more to the purpose he felt she was watching him. 'Have you anyone to go to the chemist—Enright, in Church Street?'

'My niece.'

'I'll leave a prescription there. It might ease your cramp. She could call for it later this evening. Dr. Adam Hutton is the name.'

'Aye.' And then, with a slow, broad grin, as if mocking her own taciturnity, she added, 'That's right.'

But was it taciturnity? It might be some sort of oncoming coma.

'I think I'll take your pulse again.'

As he took hold of her wrist, the cat began to purr. The pulse rate was unchanged, the pulse itself a fraction steadier.

'Well, you've got a very creditable pulse.'

The purr grew louder. He looked down at her. It ceased.

'Was that *you*?'

'I wondered when you'd notice it. It's quite tiring to do. Aren't you going to tell me I've got a creditable purr?'

Her composed expression hardened. The purr began again, easy and lulling.

'Stop it! Please stop it! You might strain your heart.'

At this, the cat sat up and examined him. Under their joint scrutiny, he somehow got out of the room. As he heard his hobbledehoy feet on the stairs, he realized that his departure had been exactly that—awkward, bashful, and incompetent, like the boy at Goatbridge; and when he reached his car, he only half believed that it was his, or that he would be able to back it out and swing into the stream of traffic.

No wonder that such women with their cats were burned for witchcraft!

*

A doctor has his professional magic, too, and by the end of the day Adam had contrived to forget about Mrs. Ackroyd. But that night, as he got into bed, he remembered how she had lain, majestic and central, and he felt a childish obligation to settle himself with equal dignity exactly in the middle of the bed. Almost instantly, he was asleep.

All that night, he dreamed of Goatbridge, only waking for long enough to be aware of this before plunging back into a further depth of dream. It was the genuine Goatbridge. He walked through the familiar streets—Crane's Lane, burrowing between the tall mills and crowed over by the stamping thud of machinery, and Union Street, with its abrupt falling perspective of mean little shops and sham-lavish barrows along the pavement edge, Technical Street and Jubilee Street, and Old Snout. And once, looking down from Old Snout, he caught sight of the canopy of smoky green and pink above the fairground and heard the steam-organ music, hot and strong, like a cough linctus. But the intensity of that bygone woe turned him aside and he went down Crab Street. There the trolley buses clanged by, the greasy brilliance of engraved and gilded glass ennobled the windows of The Dog Tavern, Dotty Jenny hurried along, whispering to herself, 'No bread at the baker's,' and outside the Labour Exchange the men of his father's generation were waiting in a queue to draw their unemployment money. But in some way all this was transparent, so that wherever he looked he saw the rise and fall of the landscape—not just in a crannied view at the end of Church Street, or desolately preserved in the bluff of rock and sickly turf above the goods yard, but everywhere manifest, shouldering itself out of houses, silent amid the clatter of machinery, sombre through the neon lights of the picture house, rough underfoot though he trod on stone pavements. And sometimes it seemed that Goatbridge was something cast by a magic lantern on the dark moorland, and at other times it seemed that the moor was welling up through Goatbridge like a gathering mist.

In the morning, he woke knowing that this dream had in some queer way enriched him. It was as though he had borrowed the Eye of Time, and by viewing Goatbridge in its simultaneity of existence and non-existence had arrived at a complete clinical observation that would at last resolve his conflict of nausea and mysterious craving. So to Mrs. Walker's inquiries as to how he had slept he replied that he had slept remarkably well.

'And you're looking well, too, if I may say so. Much better than when you came. After all, there's nothing like one's native air.'

Linda's spectacles, so clean that they were like something

in an operating theatre, flashed as she looked up. 'But, Mother, Dr. Hutton comes from the South.'

There was a twang of reproach in her voice. Mrs. Walker said nothing. Neither did he.

But how on earth had the old schemer snuffed it out?

This was Saturday. On Sunday, Linda appeared in a purple tweed tailor-made, but a providentially difficult labour spared him from seeing much of it. At Sunday supper there was another roast fowl, and Mrs. Walker remarked that one wouldn't think he'd been there only a week, he seemed quite one of the family. Linda reported that Mrs. Beaumont, encountered on the way home from evensong, had no words to express how wonderfully Dr. Hutton had put his finger on what was wrong with Delia. With intimidating frankness, Mrs. Walker asked Linda if Dr. Hutton wasn't just the co-partner that Father needed. Turning to Adam, she went on, 'I know I'd be glad to see it. I've been saying for these last five years, "James, you must take a co. or you'll be dead of overwork before you retire." Now, can't I tempt you with this nice thigh, Doctor?'

*

During Monday, Tuesday, and Wednesday, Adam began to see his results, and to plume himself on his management of patients more intricate than Miss Beaumont. He spent his spare time studying their case histories in those files that Linda's neatness made such easy reading. He began to be as the God to whom all secrets are known. The Hippocratic lust for intervenient power and insighted meddling sprouted up in him, all the stronger because he had cut it to the ground. By Wednesday midday, he was saying to himself that as he had changed his course before, he might change it again, and go back to general practice, this time not in the genteel suburban Home Counties but in some town like Mexley, where sickness and death, with a greater variety of tricks up their sleeves, would be more interesting foes to combat—though not Mexley itself, where Mrs. Walker's intentions threatened a higher price than he cared to pay. For that matter, there was also Walker, who might not match his daughter in being so very willing.

On Thursday morning, Walker's daughter, instead of knowing when she was done with, hung about the surgery, fidgeted her way as far as the door, paused, and turned back.

'I don't know how to put it, but I must. I'm afraid Mother may have annoyed you on Sunday.'

'On Sunday?'

'When she said about this being your native air. She didn't mean it unkindly—quite the contrary. It showed how much she thinks of you. But coming from the South, you might not take it that way. I've been feeling really worried about it.'

'There's nothing to worry about. As a matter of fact, your mother was partly right. I wasn't born in the South; I just happen to live there.'

And now, if she asked the obvious question, what was he going to say? But though her lips parted, it was not in inquiry. She stared at him with round eyes, her healthy, high-coloured, rawboned face remade by its expression of compassion and enlightenment, as though she had diagnosed a secret woe in him.

'Do you think that's so dreadful?' he asked.

'Well . . . Yes! Yes, I do. I can't imagine anything more wretched than to live away from one's roots. Of

29

course, it's nice to travel—I went to Switzerland once and enjoyed every moment of it. But I wouldn't have enjoyed it, it wouldn't have been like Switzerland, if I hadn't known I'd got the West Riding to come home to.'

He looked towards the window. Above the half-curtains it showed him the top of the lorry that was screaming past, the slate roofs and staring upper windows of the houses opposite, the murky sky, the whitening flashes where the wind bent the driving rain. Since the feeling her words had aroused in him was too foolish to be said, he would sing it:

'*O Bay of Dublin, my heart you're troubling,*
Your beauty haunts me like a fever dream . . .'

'Whatever you are, you're not Irish!' she exclaimed, and went away before he could stop her. Which was as well, since he had been so nearly betrayed into kissing the girl.

He had been so nearly betrayed that when he got his car out from the garage he welcomed the grime on the wind-screen and the spatters of mud on the body as though they were so many bracing admonitions to him not to make a fool of himself. All that morning, he was on the lookout for such admonitions. They did not lack. He was recognized by Mrs. Beaumont, who was wearing a transparent pink raincoat, and goodheartedly waved a small bunch of mimosa at him. He waited for ten minutes in a traffic jam while two van drivers who had collided got out of their vans and circumstantially established that the other was at fault. His roof began to leak, and he suspected he was getting a cold. But though the mimosa afforded him the pleasure of telling himself that Rome would not be like Rome if he hadn't the West Riding to get away from, he knew that he was only being toppled toward leaving, as earlier he had

been toppled toward staying. Perhaps this was what happened when one had no roots.

*

That night, Mr. Joseph Heaton, who had seemed to be
recovering, died. He was an alcoholic, a surly old bully, and
incontinent. But he was dead. At the end of the match,
death had suddenly outplayed Adam, sneaked a pawn into
the back row and made a castle of it. Adam's reaction was
to feel that he now had no alternative. He would stay, he
would root—not for any sentimental reasons but because
he wasn't going to be beat. If need were, he would marry
Linda. So he thought, eating sardine sandwiches and feeling delightfully coolheaded.

In the morning he felt coolheaded merely. But during
breakfast it seemed to him that he must have shouted these
intentions aloud and been overheard. Linda ate like one
suspended in a trance, and when he handed her the marmalade she took it as if he were worshipping her with his body
and endowing her with all his worldly goods. Mrs. Walker
said no more about Linda's excellences. Apparently, she
felt there was no further need to. In a voice that might have
been breathing o'er Eden she remarked that Dr. Walker
would be home tomorrow evening, and that it would soon
be spring. In fact, she was wondering what best to do about
the bedrooms. If he stayed on over Saturday night—and he
had given no indication to the contrary—the best bedroom
would have to be turned out on Sunday, a thing she didn't
like.

The gale had blown itself out, the rain was a drizzle. It
was a discouraging morning for a man who had made up his
mind overnight. Adam knew that his mind was made up,

but he knew more immediately that he had got a cold in his head. He would let sleeping decisions lie till the morrow, when he would talk seriously to Walker about that partnership. Meanwhile, the patients he saw on his rounds all informed him that they wouldn't be seeing him again, or that tomorrow they would be saying goodbye to him. It was irrational to resent being signed off like this; nevertheless, he resented it, and stayed longer and inquired more elaborately than he otherwise might have done. He had a long list, and in order to finish it he had to go out again after the evening surgery hours. By the time he came to Tanhouse Yard, it was so late that many windows were already lit up. The front-bedroom window of No. 11 was one of them. Well, Mrs. Ackroyd would not waste her penurious syllables on telling him she would not be seeing him again. If said at all, it would be said by him, and she would respond with an 'Aye,' or a 'That's right.'

To-day the niece was there. She opened the stairway door, and sat down again to her sewing machine.

The bedroom seemed smaller, the bed larger, the sick woman more sickly and less splendid, though she lay in the same grand attitude and held her head as erect as before. The burst of sunlight had romanticized her. The bleak gaslight stripped all that away. The cat wasn't there, either. Something else was. On the dressing table, dominating it, as she had dominated the bed, was a large photograph, a 'professional' photograph, glossy and glaring, of the head and torso of a naked woman. Her hair was heaped up on her head in a sort of casque. Her breasts were casqued in nets of sequins and imitation jewels. Slantingly across the bottom corner was printed in italic capitals *Betty d'Orsay*, 1928.

He looked from the photograph to the woman.

'You?'

'Aye. That's me.'

'You?' he said again.

'Aye. She's me, and I'm her. It was done a couple of years before the show came to Goatbridge. But I'm still her. "All Our French Artists' Models Are Alive." '

'Must you always laugh at me?' he exclaimed, and fell on his knees beside the bed, and buried his face.

'Poor Adam! You took love hard, didn't you? I never saw a boy take it harder!'

He heard her cough as her breath gave out. After a pause, she went on, 'And you telling me you were Dr. Adam Hutton! I knew you the moment you came in. I'm glad you've got on in the world.'

He rose from his knees, sat down on the bed, and took hold of her two plaits as though they were ropes to save a drowning man.

'Goatbridge Fair, eh?' she said. 'Half a dozen of us, lit up in hutches behind glass. And you came along with the rest for a sixpenny stare. Reckon you'd never seen a naked woman before.'

'I have never seen a woman since.'

'And picked on me. Poor Adam, it was the hard nut you picked. You might have got any of the others. And the letters you wrote, and the way you pestered me! You thought I was French!' she exclaimed, and began to laugh. 'You tried to talk French to me: "*Je vous aime*." '

'Why wouldn't you have me?'

'I was too young, love. If I'd been five-and-forty instead of five-and-thirty, I'd have gobbled you up, back, belly, and whiskers.'

33

'What happened to you afterwards? How did you get here? No! Don't talk! It's bad for you.'

'Well, whatever else, I didn't forget you.'

'And you got out that photograph.'

'Aye. I don't rightly know what for. But it wasn't for a tease.'

'My love, my love, I don't think that! May I undo this plait? I want to feel your hair.'

He had already begun unplaiting it. Released, her hair sprang into his hand as if to be fondled.

'Shall I purr!' she said after a while.

'Don't do anything, my darling. Lie back, and let me play with it.'

She lay back against her pillows, her hand following his through the mesh of her hair, her eyes dwelling on the photograph.

'Poor Adam!' she murmured, speaking not to him but to the woman of 1928.

' "Poor Adam!" That's what you said then, when you wouldn't have me. But now you say it better. Or I believe it more.'

'Poor Adam! Poor Bet, too! But it had to be, like. Still and all, I'm glad I got out that picture.'

'Will you give it to me?'

'I was thinking I'd have it sent you after I was dead.'

'I'd rather have it now.'

'Why not? There's some brown paper in that top left-hand drawer.'

He wrapped up the photograph, and opened his case. It was too large to go in. He stared into his case as though into another world.

'Did those pills do your cramp any good?'

'They eased it a bit.'

'I'll leave you some more. I suppose I ought to go over you.'

She saw the agonized look on his face, and cried out, 'No, no! That you won't!'

'Always the same cry. What a woman!'

'Now you must go. Oh, for goodness' sake, dust your knees! Is it to-morrow you're leaving?'

'Yes. Unless you ask me to stay. Oh, my love, my love!'

Briefly and calmly she considered it.

'You must go, lad. Best for both, this time.'

When he looked back from the stairhead, she was dreamily replaiting her hair.

*

He sat for a long time in his car, shuddering and twisting his hands, shaken not by this classical grief of the present but by the untamed remembrance of his former woe. A prostitute was walking up and down, and presently she came and tapped on the glass. He shook his head, and started the car. He was at a loss where to go, or how to get through the next few hours, till a sneeze reminded him that he had a cold, and could make it a pretext for going straight to bed.

On Saturday, Dr. Walker, getting his full pound of flesh, arrived late in the afternoon, as Adam had done a fortnight earlier.

'Hullo, hullo! Well, here I am, safe back in time for tea, and how are you all? Hullo, Hutton, everything gone all right?' Without waiting for an answer, he turned to his wife. 'Ada! I've got a piece of news for you. Splendid news. But I must have a cup of tea before anything else.

35

I haven't tasted a decent cup of tea since I left home. Cat-lap!'

He poured the tea down his wiry gullet, handed back the cup to be refilled, rubbed his knees, and announced, 'Ada, I've got a partner. I met him at the hotel, he was lunching there. He'd come to Llangibby for his aunt's funeral—from Scotland, the deuce of a way to come for an aunt!—and was travelling back that same night. Well, we got to talking, I took to him, he took to me. So far, he's a trainee-assistant with a view—at some place near Peebles, with a sulphur spa—but there wasn't enough future for him. I soon found out that what he wanted was to come south and see the world. Come to Mexley, I said. We've got a bit of everything, even anthrax. Of course, he's never had an anthrax, and his eyes positively sparkled. Nice-looking fellow, too, and quite young. His name's Maclaren, and he's coming to have a look round next week. So there you are, and I hope you're pleased, Ada.'

Mrs. Walker said it was the very news she'd been hoping for, and that she rather believed Mrs. Beaumont had had a grandmother who went to a spa in Scotland—though she couldn't say what was wrong with her.

'Nothing at all, if she was like the rest of that family. And Linda, my girl, cut me a slice of cake, and get ready to find a nice little house for him. Not too far out. Or a maisonette. Lodgings won't do, because of the children. Didn't I say he was a married man? Well, he is. And an anaesthetist. Just the very thing we want. Well, now, Hutton, let's get down to it. Any deaths?'

'Joseph Heaton.'

Linda was toasting herself a crumpet at the fire. Her hand was steady, her face composed. Only when the crumpet fell off the toasting fork and she was so slow to retrieve it could one have guessed that her thoughts were sad and elsewhere. Poor Linda, Adam thought, one blow on top of another, rat-tat! It was as though he had glanced out of his own tragedy and seen the sawdust trickling from a doll.

An hour later, he was driving south over the same route he had come by.

THE FIFTH OF NOVEMBER

Feeling the need for a little repose and luxury, Ellie, on her way back from the carpet factory where she worked, turned aside into the church of St. Mary Ragmarket. She had done so before at various times, and could enter without feeling constrained to put on any particular behaviour, to bow the knee and adapt the heart to the presence of a ciborium that, wrapped in a striped veil, presented a rather Turkish appearance, to avoid the melancholy stare of the figure on the cross, to admire the architecture, or to apprehend interruption. The church stood in the old part of the town, whose venerable slums were in process of being cleared away and replaced by industrial buildings. The fairground from which it took its name was now occupied by a bus depot, and the remaining streets and alleyways did not house a church-going population. Though St. Mary Ragmarket had been the parish church of one of the Pilgrim Fathers, whose ancestors knelt among the emblazoned figures in its armorial east window, and as such was visited by a certain number of pilgrim Americans, the proportion of American visitors in a town like Thorpe is small at any time, smaller still in November; and at 6 p.m. on a November evening any American visitor would be pursuing livelier interests. Ellie could feel pretty sure of having the church to herself.

The door closed behind her, and the noises of traffic, though still audible, passed into a different dimension of sound. Her sense of hearing relaxed. Her eyes recovered

from the joggle of dark streets and devouring headlights.
She saw instead the composed clear-obscure of the dimly
lit interior, where, as if she were a fish in a pool, the dark
pews, the glimmering effigies, the blackness of the glass in
the traceried windows surrounded her like rocks and
fronded waterweeds. But when she sighed with relief, no
bubble rose to the surface. Nothing corroborated her sigh.

As she expected, the church was pleasantly warm.
Warmth is one of the outward signs of the variety of
English churchmanship known as High—an atmosphere
in which ciboriums, images of the Blessed Virgin, sanctuary
lamps, stands for holding votive candles, and shallow
wadded mats referred to as 'kneelers' are in their natural
clime. In churches known as Low one finds, instead of
kneelers, hassocks, which themselves are high. It varies
inversely. Ellie knew all this, not because she was religiously
inclined but because, in the days before calamity forced her
down in the world, she had been on the fringe of the class
called educated, with a mind sufficiently at leisure to enjoy
noticing things, and speculating over them, and reading
books from the public library in order to learn more exactly
about them. But this was a long time ago, and the scraps of
knowledge she had then accumulated lay like a heap of
dead leaves, broomed away into an unfrequented corner of
her mind and only stirring now and then, and only the
lightest and least significant of them stirring, at that. The
Reformation of the English Church had come about, men
had burned at the stake and a faith as fiery had blown the
flames, Jesuit missionaries had been disembowelled at
Tyburn, Laud's hands had fluttered in blessing through
the prison grate, Quakers had been whipped through the
streets, Newman had torn himself weeping from the

mother he abjured, and as a result of all this anguish and altercation Ellie knew that St. Mary Ragmarket could be relied on to provide warmth, repose, and a sense of luxury.

They were being provided as usual, and with them the amplitude of the nave, the remoteness of the roof, a serene faint smell of wax polish and candle wax, an uncluttered spaciousness; but to-night, for some reason, the quiet and the solitude had taken on a different quality, and were silence and emptiness. No building had ever been so totally silent, so totally uninhabited. It was as if the fabric had grown up, and endured through the centuries, without any-one ever knowing about it or ever coming here. It was as though it were unvisitable, like a place in a dream, a dream into which she had got by mistake and out of which she would never pass. Perhaps the difference lay in herself. For to-night, though her body was relaxing like a cat on a familiar hearth, her mind would not relax. It was as though she were waiting, helplessly, ignorantly, rigidly waiting—as during the air-raid winters one had waited—for some dreadful thing that was about to declare itself, some inevit-able, shattering recognition that would presently explode from within her. She ransacked her memory for a possible cause—a tap left running, a bill unpaid. She ran through the familiar rota of familiar dreads—Mother dying, herself taken ill and carted off to hospital, the rent raised, her job lost, another war, a purely hypothetical illegitimate son of Father's, specious and bullying, turning up to prey on them. There was no quiver of response. It must be nerves. For everything was just as usual. Her day had been no more tiring or uncongenial than usual. She was going home, as usual, where as usual she would get supper and serve it to Mother in her wheelchair, talk for a while, put

THE FIFTH OF NOVEMBER

her to bed, wash up, set things to rights, and go to bed herself, with the door ajar, so that she would wake up at any call from the adjoining room. Other women led lives quite as restricted, and much sadder, having no one to love. She had her mother, who, together with the habit of love, had survived thirty years of poverty and had been, till only a short while ago, a supporting and even a reviving person to go home to. For it was only in these last few years—four years, six years?—when deafness had closed her in, and given her the stunned, inattentive expression it was so painful to see, that acquaintances had begun to say she was wonderful for her age, and quite a character, and that Ellie would feel quite lost when she passed on.

This was the sort of acquaintance they were now reduced to—people who thirty years ago would only have been deserving old dears for Mother to give port wine and blankets to, people to whom it would be inconceivable that thirty years ago Mother walked on three-inch heels with the gait of a queen, subjugated everyone she met, and could kiss the wall behind her. Then, too, she was wonderful for her age—but no one would have dared say so. This was the being whom Father deserted, going off with a smug slut whose petticoats dangled below her skirts. 'I can do without him,' Mother had declared. 'Alimony is as good as matrimony at my age.' It was a brave boast, and while the alimony lasted, it held. Then, during the slump, he died, penniless. She mourned him briefly and tempestuously, and afterward began to pick holes in him.

Poor Mother!

It was time to think of getting back to her. Pauses for repose and luxury in St. Mary Ragmarket seldom exceeded ten minutes, and to-night, since St. Mary Ragmarket was not living up to Ellie's expectations, there was the less reason to linger there. Yet she wanted to linger; or rather, she was reluctant to quit it for streets where she would certainly encounter more of those horrible Guys. It was the Fifth of November, and at every turn she had met groups of children bearing their dummy towards the bonfire, on a chair or in a handcart, and assailing her with, 'Penny for the Guy.' It was curiously shocking to be confronted with these effigies, stuffed with straw, bedizened in human rags, sagging forward over the string that fastened them by the waist to their conveyance. It was mortifying not to be able to spare the penny. As she walked on, the chant pursued her like a hail of pebbles:

> *'Guy, Guy, hit him in the eye!*
> *Hang him on a lamp-post and never let him die.'*

Nevertheless, she rose and went to the door. As she opened it, she heard a spurt of sound, the sizzling uprush of a rocket, an outburst of young yells. Then a voice said, 'Now for the squibs!' Remembering the squib that had burned a hole in her stocking, she drew back into the church; and to kill time and combat the sense of silence and emptiness, she began a tour of examination. Presently she came to the stand for votive candles. It was an iron frame supporting three tiers of branching sockets. All were empty. Only a few had remnants of candle grease in them, and in these, as she discovered by poking, the grease was hardened and quite cold. Below was a platform, and on it were candles in a container, a box of matches, a few match ends, and a slotted box fastened to the stand by a chain and lettered 'CANDLES FOURPENCE EACH.' Fourpence apiece for such puny specimens! No wonder the sockets were empty.

Even while this reflection was passing through her mind, she had dropped four pennies into the box and taken a candle.

Though what does one burn a candle for, and to whom, and why? What deity or demiurge did she think to invoke? Certainly not that presiding white plaster Virgin near by, to which she had taken an instant dislike because its expression of pigheaded meekness recalled the woman Father had gone off with. Not God, that Maker and Manager of all things visible and invisible, of whom it is declared by the Prophets that He is above the heavens, and who is therefore, presumably, above bribes. And on whose behalf—her luckless own, her irremediable mother's? And why? Out of all the things that can be done for fourpence—still, in spite of the rise in the cost of living, quite a considerable number —why pick on this?

Meanwhile, she was painstakingly fixing the candle to stand firm and upright. When it was settled to her satisfaction, she struck a match and held the flame to the wick, which after a momentary halfheartedness took fire and began to burn independently. Oh, no need to ask why! The answer was in the act. The dated confident little flame, the minute dated warmth, the wax gently yielding—by bringing this about she had brought a new light and a new warmth into the cavernous world. She had created an impersonal good, a good that would benefit no one and harm no one, impose no obligation and fulfil no duty. Looking at her candle, now burning so diligently and composedly, she felt a kind of delighting trust in it. How far it spread its beams! How pleased it looked! How bravely it burned, the phoenix of its kind, among those yawning empty sockets! She had another four pennies; and although

eightpence is two-thirds of a shilling, which is the economic
unit of a slot meter, yet, if only out of gratitude—gratitude
for having experienced a purity of gratitude such as she had
not felt since childhood—she must light a second candle, a
votive candle to the first. She tried it in one socket and
another, to see where it looked best. When this was
decided on, and the candle firmly established, she struck a
match. As if she had provoked an echo, there came from
outside an answering spurt, a rushing sizzle as the rocket
tore upwards, a thud.

The match burned unheeded in her hand. Only when it
scorched her finger did she throw it down.

With a spurt and a sizzle and a thud, a realization had
exploded in her mind. Those dummies, those frightful
pitiable dummies! They were exhibitions to her of what
her mother was becoming, had almost become. The horror
they aroused in her only corroborated and proclaimed an
abhorrence she had not dared to admit. It was with abhorrence that she now looked at her mother. Abhorrence must
have been there for months, disguised as a flinching pity.
And now, knowing the truth, she must go home and
experience it.

She lit the second candle, stared at its magicless flame,
and went to the back of the church, where it was darkest
and sternest, to sit for a while longer. She would be late.
Mother, clutching at her last pleasure, a nice hot supper
with something tasty, would be angry at having been kept
waiting. She would scold, in her flat voice, and afterwards
she would weep. She was eighty-four; hunger, suspicion,
and self-pity was all that was left to spice her dreary days.
Ellie, telling herself that she must somehow scratch up a
handful of courage—or if not courage, compassion, and if

not compassion, common sense—sat waiting for the candles to burn out. The first died easily. The second flared and struggled. After this, there was no excuse to remain. She remained, sitting bolt upright, her head gradually drooping forward.

*

She became conscious of a stir of cold air, and heard foot-steps approaching. She did not move. The footsteps slowed, drew level with her, and halted, creaking slightly. She did not look up, but out of the corner of her eye she saw a straight black garment reaching to the floor—a cassock, and within the cassock, no doubt, a rector. He coughed, drew breath to speak, thought better of it, coughed again, again drew a breath.

'Good evening! Jolly of you to come in like this.'

She made no reply. After a moment or two, he moved on. She stumbled to her feet and hurried out of the building, knowing that never again would she set foot in it.

When the door had closed behind her, he gave a move-ment of the shoulders that could have been a shrug if habit had not made it an acknowledgment of a burden. Once again he had done the wrong thing. He had spoken when he should have kept silence. Surely, there had never been a visitor more patently in need of a kind word than this poor old girl, so gaunt and derelict, her bony, coarsened hands clamped on her shabby handbag. But it had been the wrong thing. He had offended her, and she had fluttered away like some ungainly bird. Perhaps a notice in the porch saying, as much to him as to others, 'Persons entering this Church will not be spoken to' . . . Better phrased, of course. If by some extraordinary chance—a forgotten glove (but had those hands ever been gloved?), a change of heart—she were to return . . . But she did not return.

His purpose resumed him. He went to the altar rail, knelt down, and began to pray for the soul of Guy Fawkes.

A QUESTION OF DISPOSAL

'AND he went away like that—holding my hand.' At this point in her narrative Bell Kirby burst into tears.

Mr. Kirby's other children—his sons, Walter and Clive, his married daughters, Eva and Lily—felt as if they were hearing about the death of some father not their own.

Long ago they had made their escape from him, the sons by getting on in the world, the daughters by marrying. Summoned to his deathbed by identical telegrams of 'DAD DYING COME AT ONCE BELL,' and all arriving too late for it, they were back among the familiar objects of their youth, though not in their birthplace. Ten years previously, Edwin Kirby had sold his farm and bought a villa on the outskirts of the market town. He had insisted on bringing all the furniture. It crowded the small rooms and narrow passages, looking much bulkier, not seeming much shabbier, and sounding exactly the same—the tick of the grandfather's clock, which had slow-marched between his inquiries and their halting replies, the twang that went off in the sofa, the machine-gun rattle of the roll-top desk. Bell had opened the desk, and instantly the old sense of resentful, terrified, destroying tedium had swept over Lily like a dirty flood. Oh, Lord, to think of those years! And Bell, left alone with him, had endured so many more of them. Poor Bell!

'Here it is,' said Bell, with her grating Midlands accent. (It had been a surprise to find that Bell's accent was still tied to the soil.) 'Here it is. Dad cut it out of the paper at the time. "Local Octogenarian Recalls Former Days." Up till then, I'd never known how old he was.'

She read aloud an interview in which her father had expressed his views on modern farming, keeping the sharpest lash for the last. ' *"It's not natural,"* concluded *Mr. Kirby with a hearty chuckle, "so I suppose it's artistic."* '

The hale old taunt, read from the yellowing newspaper in a voice where the original tones seemed to have lingered and grown sallow, had too much life in it. Killed adders do not die till sundown. Edwin Kirby was still upstairs, waiting to be coffined. The silence was broken by Eva, exclaiming, 'Well, Bell, now he's gone you might at least get rid of that spittoon.'

Bell put back the cutting. Down came the lid of the desk with the same rattle and snap, and Lily wondered how Clive, who had been the greatest sufferer among them, could sit there so tranquilly reading the *Collected Works* of Eliza Cook.

'All I can say is, Eva, there's not many left like that nowadays.'

'Too true.'

When Edwin Kirby was about to lose his temper, his left eyelid would twitch convulsively. Bell's eyelid was now doing the same. Walter coughed warningly, and once again conveyed Eileen's regrets that her poor health would prevent her from coming to the funeral.

'I didn't ask her, did I? I didn't ask any of the in-laws, and didn't expect to see them. . . . Who's that?'

The gate had clicked and a man was coming up the path. Calm settled on Bell's eyelid. 'It's the coal man. And if he thinks I'm going to pay full price for the stuff he brought last time, half slate and half slack, he's mistaken. As he'll soon learn.' She hurried out.

The coal man must have been accustomed to being disillusioned, for he was heard retorting with spirit.

Eva lit a cigarette. Walter, yawning, said, 'Two days before the funeral. Two very long days.'

'No need for you and Clive to complain. You're sleeping at The George. What about Lily and me, squeezed into a back bedroom along with that awful wardrobe he used to lock us into when he went out for the evening? "Safe bind, safe find." Do you remember, Lily?'

'Don't! I can't bear to think of it. Or of poor Bell.'

That commiseration would have been better left unspoken just then. Their sense of guilt towards Bell which, severally borne, weighed pretty lightly, had become immeasurably heavier and guiltier now that they were reunited. It seemed as though they had plotted together to sacrifice her to their father, whereas in fact each in turn had done no more than thankfully get away.

The conversation on the doorstep had taken a different turn. Bell was relating, the coal man condoling.

'And he went away like that—holding my hand.'

Eva grimaced. 'I shall go out of my mind if I hear that again. Anyone would think she was wound up. Besides, I don't believe a word of it.'

'If it's any comfort to her, poor Bell! . . . '

'Lily, for heaven's sake . . . You're as bad as she is. Can't you say anything but "poor Bell"?'

'She'll get over it, once he's underground,' remarked Walter.

'But she'll still be with us.'

Clive's voice was so impersonal that he seemed to be

49

reading these words aloud from Eliza Cook as a text upon which a sermon would follow. They sighed in acquiescence, and settled themselves as congregations do; but at that moment Bell reappeared. Tears still trickled over her flat pale face.

'Well, I've given him a piece of my mind, and I don't think he'll forget it. And what do you think he had the impertinence to say to me? He said . . .'

She recounted the altercation, and went on to recount other altercations with other tradesmen. Except that occasionally the names of the tradesmen were new to them, it was very much like the evenings when Dad came home from those monthly days of wrath when he stayed on after the market closed to settle bills and distribute pieces of his mind.

On the plea of something they really must watch on television, Walter and Clive got away before supper. When they had gone, Bell invited her sisters upstairs for another view of the corpse. They had no wish for this but recognizing a clammy impulse of hospitality they yielded. The rest of the evening was spent in discussing the funeral. 'I've only asked a few,' said Bell. 'The Cooksons, Aunt Het, Cousin Lamb. And Sally Spicer. I owe it to her, really, she was so obliging that time when I had shingles, though she's as soppy as they're made. Anyhow, she won't come. Can't afford to. And I'm not going to put myself out getting them a great meal. I'm not equal to it, after all I've been through.'

Late that night, still hesitating to undress and get into the gaunt bed, Eva and Lily sat warming themselves with sups of whiskey from Eva's flask and trying to talk of anything but the reason why they were there.

'I've never actually tasted vodka, have you?' Lily said.

'No. What's it made of?'

'Well, I have heard that it's partly made from toad-stools. But I can't believe it.'

'People will say anything, won't they?'

Conversation soon became even harder to keep up, for Bell had begun to snore. Lily surrendered to the present. 'What a ghastly noise! Still, it shows she's asleep. I'm sure she must need it.'

'She was always a snorer.'

'All that talk about what she's been through. . . .Do you suppose she means Dad dying, or what it was like before?'

'Dad dying. And isn't she making the most of it, too? As for what it was like before, it's my opinion she didn't mind it.'

'Eva! Live with Dad and not mind it? It's just not pos-sible. Besides, think of her letters.'

'People always rush to write letters when they've got something to complain of. And I'll tell you this much, Lily. Bell gives me the creeps. She's got like him.'

'I can tell you worse than that. It's been weighing on me ever since I arrived. You know I got here first. Well, before I could say a word, she threw her arms round my neck, fit to throttle me, and she said, "Now you're all I've got left. You and Eva and Walter and Clive are all I've got in the world." Well, you see what that could mean. She'll want to live with one or other of us. And she *is* our sister.'

'That's all right.' Eva got up and began to undress. 'Sup-pose she does, the answer's quite simple. Clive's the only unmarried one, and Clive will have to have her. What's more, he knows it.'

'Knows it?'

'In his bones he does. Didn't you notice how quiet he was?'

'And sat reading all the time?'

'Exactly! Come on, get your things off. It's nearly midnight.'

'It will be like old times, sleeping in the same bed.'

'Thank God it isn't!'

They lay side by side, each pretending to be asleep, each wakefully conscious of the dead man lying voiceless and unnaturally clean in the adjoining room, each oppressed by Bell's loud, desolate snores, which broke on the silence of the house like waves breaking on a pebble beach.

*

At breakfast there were several letters of condolence to be handed round and commented on. The undertaker came, the corpse was coffined and taken away, and after this the three sisters went out to order their wreaths and do some shopping. In every shop Bell recounted how her father had gone away holding her hand, and burst into tears. Brothers and sisters met at a restaurant for lunch, to save Bell the trouble of cooking. It had been agreed that each should pay his own share, but when the bill came Walter insisted on paying for Bell.

'It's very kind of you, I'm sure. But what a nerve to ask seven and sixpence for such a poor meal! Still, it's the same everywhere. These last years, I've been put to all manner of shifts to keep the household bills from Dad.'

'How on earth did you do it?' asked Eva.

'Well, now he's gone I don't mind telling you. I'd go to two grocers, you see, two butchers, and only show him the one set of bills.'

Walter remarked that Bell ought to be Chancellor of the Exchequer. Then, since the moment seemed suitable, he went on in a carefully incurious voice, 'Have you any idea how he's left things?'

'Fifty pounds for the funeral. And the house and furniture come to me.'

'Quite right, too. Well, what else?'

'I don't reckon there'll be much else. It was all in the annuity. Didn't you know about the annuity?'

None of them had known about the annuity.

'And did he suppose you'd live in the house and eat the furniture?' inquired Clive.

'Eat the furniture? Oh—a joke. No, I was to sell up, you see.'

Her glance flicked from one to another. It was anxious, slightly challenging, and yet sly. Clive said, 'Yes, I see.'

The question was, *did* Clive see? Did he realize that not only would Bell live with him but that he would have to support her? Lily, feeling like an unrehearsed assassin, clutched at Eva as they left the restaurant, and muttered that it was going to be rather awkward, wasn't it? Eva replied that the first thing to be done was to get Bell out of the way. As soon as they were back, she noticed that Bell was looking tired, and urged her to go and lie down. Walter added that Eileen always lay down in the afternoon, by doctor's orders. Bell, remarking that anybody would think they wanted to get rid of her, rejected the idea. Lily said that Bell looked pale, she really did. Pallor is a politer imputation than fatigue.

'I dare say I do. I don't paint,' said Bell.

Then, as though repenting of this thrust, she began

inquiring after her nephews and nieces, and asked Lily if she had brought any snapshots of the twins. This presently led to a family photograph album, into which Bell had stuck every photograph she had received of the younger generation. There were not many of these, but when they were exhausted she turned back to the earlier pages. The album was meticulously kept: everything in it was firmly and squarely gummed in place, and identified and dated. Demises had been added whenever occasion arose. 'I like to keep it up to date,' she remarked.

'You are our recording angel, Bell,' said Clive, voicing the feelings of all their hearts. 'We are a very ugly family,' he added.

'I can't help that. You're all I've got. I look at you on Sunday evenings.'

Her words called up a vision of such destitute boredom that they remained speechless. This apparently placated her, for she asked if they would like ham with their tea. Tea was at five. When she went out to prepare it, they drew closer. But before anyone had spoken, the door opened and Bell looked in to ask if they were sure they didn't want ham. After this, she went on reappearing, bringing in a tablecloth, and then a smaller tablecloth to lay across it, and then the teapot stand, and then, by bits and pieces, the crockery and the food, finally coming in empty-handed to stare at the table in case there was something she had forgotten.

There was a knock on the front door. Hope bounded in Eva's breast, for perhaps this was another tradesman to be given a piece of Bell's mind. The front door was opened, and then slammed. Bell came in crumpling a telegram. 'Of all the extravagance! It's from Sally Spicer, if you please.

"Feel for you so deeply shall be at the church." The girl's a fool if ever there was one. Not that she's much of a girl. Forty if she's a day. I remember . . .'

Tea was nearly over, Bell was still on the trail of Sally Spicer's exact age, when again the gate opened and a woman carrying a large box came up the path. Bell leaped up, exclaiming, 'At last!' It was the dress she had ordered for the funeral.

When she and the dressmaker had gone upstairs for the final trying-on, Walter leaned back, settled his waistcoat, drew a deep breath, and surveyed them like a chairman. Less like a chairman, he began, 'That damned old fox, that damned, artful, selfish old crocodile! An annuity!'

'And after she'd given up her whole life to him. Poor Bell!'

'It's most extraordinary that she didn't mention it to any of us.'

'She was always very close.'

'Of course, she might have something put away. But it couldn't be much.'

'Or he might have kept something by, when he bought the annuity.'

'Not a hope!'

'Not a hope,' agreed Clive. 'He just went away—holding her hand. He always got slightly sentimental after he'd thrashed us.'

'The queer thing is, she doesn't seem in the least worried about it.' Walter spoke these words with particular gloom.

'Oh, what's the use of beating round the bush like this?' exclaimed Eva. 'She'll be down at any moment, and we've got to get something settled. Bell isn't worried because she means to live with one or other of us. She told Lily so—didn't she, Lily?'

'The moment I got into the house,' said Lily dejectedly.

'So there you are, Clive! You're the unmarried one and you'll have to have her. It stands to reason.'

'I don't deny it's reasonable. But I don't think she could stand the climate.'

'The climate? What's wrong with the east coat? It's bracing.'

'The Gold Coast in West Africa. The white man's grave. I am being sent there to experiment with one of the firm's new insecticides. I leave in ten days' time, and I expect to be there for five years. . . . I see you don't believe me.'

He laid a letter on the table. It acknowledged his acceptance, and was dated a fortnight back.

Bell and the dressmaker were coming downstairs, and the dressmaker was urging Bell to bear up.

'Well, I'm sure we ought to congratulate you,' said Walter.

Bell entered, and a strong smell of recent gin entered with her. 'It's a perfect fit,' she said, and burst into tears. The sight of herself in total black had been too much for her nerves; the gin had been too much for her feelings. During the rest of the evening she was maudlin, quarrelsome, and clinging as a leech.

*

A little before dawn, Lily nudged her sister. 'Eva. Are you asleep?'

'Asleep? What a question to ask when I've been lying here for hours on end racking my brains how to work on

Walter— And then when I'm just dozing off, you dig me in the ribs to ask if I'm asleep. Have a heart!'

'Listen. I've just remembered that Sally Spicer's coming to the funeral.'

'Well, we can't stop her, can we? Yah-ah-oo! This ghastly bed! I wish Clive was in it. Sally Spicer, too, for all I care.'

'*She will be.*'

'Always bicycling, wasn't she? Hat like a Noah's ark.'

'Wake up, Eva! I'll pinch you.'

'Yah-ah-oo . . . Ow! Oh, my good God, what a night! Now, what's all this about Sally Spicer?'

'You'll soon see. I've been racking my brains, too, and what with Bell making a night of it and you dozing off, as you call it, I got so frantic that I got out of bed and went down on my knees and prayed. "Good Lord, deliver us," I said. I must have said it twenty times.'

'Well? Anything come of it?'

'And then, just like a vision, I saw Sally Spicer standing by an open grave, in a sky-blue plastic mac. She's the answer. She's the one to live with Bell. She's got no relations, she has nothing coming to her, she lives in lodgings, her only interest in life is getting mixed up with lame dogs. I tell you, she's made for it!'

Eva sat up. 'I do believe you've hit on something. But it's going to take managing. We must think it out. . . . I'm going to turn on the light.'

The unshaded light shone down on the two middle-aged women—Eva with her tousled crop, Lily with her long thin plaits—and on the rumpled bed with its same mean, bluish blankets they had lain under in their girlhood. Their cheeks were flushed, their eyes were beady, and they conversed in rapid undertones, as they had done when their father was alive and his snores had been their warrant of a precarious safety.

*

By the time they got up, they had decided to keep Sally Spicer to themselves. For it was they who were really menaced. Clive was safe out of it—anyway, Clive had never been reliable—and Walter could be so sure that Mrs. Walter wouldn't endure Bell for more than a week that he was not likely to feel himself seriously endangered. It was later, Lily urged, when it came to stumping up, that Walter would come into the picture.

'All the same, Walter might be useful. He's a man, and if Bell turned awkward . . .'

'Heavens alive, it mustn't come to that! It must be Sally's idea, and Sally must do the persuading. All we've got to do is to put the idea into Sally's head, and make her think she thought of it, and then see that she goes the right way about it, and doesn't run off on any lame-dogging or ministering-angeling. Bell wouldn't mind being a Brave Miss Lonelyheart, but as for being a Lame Dog, it would be fatal.'

'It's going to be nice and easy,' said Eva.

'It will need tact, of course. That's why I don't want Walter in it.'

Wholly thankful, if slightly dubious, Eva submitted to this brand-new aspect of Lily—a demonstration indeed of what can be wrought by prayer. Lily's confidence so far infected her that when Walter and Clive came in after breakfast she was momentarily taken aback because they looked no less gloomy than they had looked overnight. She was even more taken aback when Walter remarked, 'Well, by this afternoon we shall know;' for her mind was so occupied by Lily's project that she could only suppose he had somehow got wind of it.

But Lily, quick as a flash, replied, 'I've never heard a will read out. I hope I shan't be silly and cry.'

Quick as a flash, too, when they entered the church, Lily spotted Sally Spicer—who in actual fact was wearing not a sky-blue plastic mac but a grey coat and skirt—detached herself from the rest, squeezed Sally's hand, and whispered, 'I know why you're here. You've always been such a good friend to Bell. It will mean just everything to her.' And though at that moment Bell turned a raking glance on them and said peremptorily, 'Oh, come on, Lily, what on earth are you dawdling for?' Sally Spicer continued to look tremulously gratified.

The grave had been dug in the new part of the cemetery —for as Mr. Kirby's wife had run away from him and shortly afterwards committed suicide there was no marital grave to be reopened for him. The sight of this part of the cemetery imposed a common reflection on all his returning children: that it was so very much fuller than when they last saw it. It was also instructively plain that the relations and family friends standing in a little group by the graveside were correspondingly as much readier to be buried themselves. A fragmentary youthfulness still clung to Sally Spicer, but only as if it were some faded, out-of-date garment she had never been prosperous enough to replace. It won't do, thought Eva. Bell would tear her up in a twelvemonth, and then it will have to be faced all over again. Poor little creature, it was really a shame. She gazed at Sally with such compassion that Sally became conscious of the gaze, looked round, blushed, and quivered. Lily whispered, 'Splendid! Well done, Eva! She's certainly hooked.'

When they returned to the house, Bell, who had gone through the funeral with sturdy decorum, began to show signs of nervous tension. She opened windows and shut them again, straightened the vases on the mantelshelf, and wound the clock. Presently the chosen funeral guests reassembled. There would be the reading of the will, and a cold meal, but before these events convention demanded a small show of conversation. Lily was Aunt Het's godchild, and had expectations. Nevertheless, she imperilled them by breaking away from an account of Aunt Het's shortened breath in order to show Sally Spicer a bird's nest in the back garden. When they reappeared, she gave a slight nod. Eva got up and grasped Sally's hand. The three sat down entwined on the window seat. A silence fell. Mr. Raven, the solicitor, drew his chair to the table, produced a long envelope, and glanced towards the group on the window seat. Sally Spicer rose, but Lily pulled her down again. 'I'm sure Sally can stay, Mr. Raven. We've always looked on her as one of the family.' Mr. Raven remarked, as though to condone this slight informality, that the reading of the will would not take him long. It did not. Edwin Kirby had appointed Cuthbert Raven and Wilfred Cookson as his executors, directing that each should receive ten pounds for his trouble. He bequeathed his gold watch to his nephew Cecil Emmanuel Lamb, his plated inkstand to his sister Henrietta Budge, five pounds apiece to his sons Walter and Clive, his daughters Eva and Lily, and the residue of his estate, less fifty pounds to pay for his funeral, to his daughter Rosabella.

Having read the will, Mr. Raven gave a noncommittal cough.

'How much capital did my father leave?' asked Clive.

'In fact, not very much. In fact, so far as I can ascertain, a sum of one hundred and nineteen pounds. As no doubt you are aware, he had bought an annuity.'

Clive took out a five-pound note. 'Here you are, Bell. That settles that. You can count on me for a hundred a year.'

'Now, that is very right and proper,' said Mr. Raven. 'And if Miss Kirby will allow me, I will follow Mr. Clive Kirby's example as regards my executor's solatium.'

Mr. Cookson said he would do the same.

'Walter?' said Clive.

'I will, of course, pay the funeral expenses,' said Walter. 'As for the future, I am not so free as my brother. I have a family. But I will look into it, and do what I can.'

'So will we,' said Eva and Lily.

'Well, thank you all,' said Bell. 'I shall be glad of it, I'm sure. Now, Sally, since you're here, you can help me bring in the refreshments.'

Sally's hot, bony hand quivered like an unfledged bird in Eva's grasp.

'Not yet, Bell, not yet! I've got something to say, too. I can't do much, but I'll do what I can. Bell, I've made up my mind. Don't think you're to be left all alone, for I'm coming to live with you and look after you. And what money I have, we'll share it. I won't be a burden, I eat next to nothing, and my poor old dog's dead. I'll come to-morrow.'

'You can come to-morrow, and welcome. But you can't stop more than a week, for after that there won't be a bedroom for you. I've got an elderly couple called Pollen coming into the front room, I'm putting two single beds into my own room, for a pair of young ladies who are friends and work at the boot factory, so they'll be out all day, and I'm moving myself into the small room at the back. So you see, what with that and making over the front parlour as more of a lounge, like, I shall have plenty to do these next few days, and it will be very convenient to have you lending a hand.'

'Very well. I'll come to-morrow.'

'What's more, since everyone's so generous, I'll pay for your ticket.'

'Thank you, Bell.'

It was Cecil Lamb who made the first comment, remarking, 'You seem to have got it all planned out.'

'Yes, I have.'

Aunt Het said, 'It strikes me, my girl, that you must have got busy with some of this before your Dad passed away.'

'Yes, Aunt Het, I did. I knew what would happen if I wasn't beforehand with it. Once bit, twice shy. After all those years with Dad, I wanted a life of my own. I knew what it would be, otherwise. "You must come to us, now, dear Bell. We'll make a home for you. You'll soon fit into our ways, and there's a lot of work left in you yet." The only thing I didn't know was which of the four it would be. And judging from the way they kept looking at each other, and making excuses to get me out of the room, they were still arguing about it themselves. I dare say in the end they'd have been casting lots for me. But you won't get me now,' she exclaimed, turning on her brothers and sisters. 'No, you won't get me. I've foxed you, one and all.'

62

BARNBY ROBINSON

'REMEMBER,' she said to him, in the voice of last words, 'remember, if ever you need me, if you are ill, if—anyway, remember, I shall be here, just as usual.'

'Of course I shall remember; and probably I shall often be back, fetching books or boots or something. Besides, for all I know, in six months I shall be back in Sawbridge for good. I wish you'd get it into your head that this is just experimental.'

She shook her head, as if she were driving away any such hovering thought. He looked round the room. His expression was sullen and distracted. She looked round the room, too. On both their parts it was an expedient not to look at each other. Her expression was resigned, but contained a hint of dawning purpose. Once it was over, once he was out of the house, she would attend to the cactuses, which were positively drooping—even they, untouched by emotional complications—from drought and neglect.

'So goodbye for now, Melissa.'

'Goodbye.'

From the passage he said, raising his voice, 'And you remember, too. If you want me, if anything goes wrong with Judy, if either of you is ill, you're to let me know at once. See?'

Driving to the station in a taxi (for Melissa was to retain the car), watching the familiar, nice-minded little suburban dwellings flick by, Barnby Robinson remarked with a groan, 'Oh Lord God, how awful that was! But she'll do far better without me.' In less than an hour he would be in London, embracing Molly and going out to lunch.

*

Melissa went into the kitchen, where the coffee Barnby had refused as a stirrup cup was still warm. But she wanted more than coffee. She fetched the remainder of last night's carrot soup from the larder and began spooning it out of the pot. Like all her soups, it was home-made, nourishing, and excellent.

In the letter to Judy—thanks to a godmother's legacy so providentially cloistered in a boarding school—she would mention amongst other items of home news (the next-door cat's kittens, the new bathroom curtains made from the old blue bedspread) Daddy's departure for London, where for the next few months he would be too busy with the play he was writing for Miss Cullen to come home much, if at all. Later on, Sawbridge could be told in cool, twentieth-century tones, 'Barnby and I feel we might be happier if we lived apart;' from which would presently develop, 'I'm sure it's better for Barnby, at any rate. Artists don't really want home life, you know—or they think they don't.' At a further stage in this imaginary conversation, some unspecified third party intervened who had met Barnby and been struck—shocked, even—to see him looking so ill and uncared-for. This glimpse into the healing future coincided with the last spoonfuls of the soup. Whatever Molly Cullen could or could not be to Barnby, she could not be a source of nourishment. *Barnby says your cooking is blissful.* (The rolling voice and rolling eyes had lost nothing from cold storage in Melissa's memory.) *Cookery is my fondest dream, but all I know how to do is fudge and omelettes.* Fudge and omelettes!

Write to Judy; then tidy the sitting room. Then lunch, which had better be macaroni *au gratin,* since she had forgotten to cut down the daily order for milk—a proof of what Barnby's departure had meant to her. After lunch, she would walk to the dairy, enjoying the fresh air and saving a telephone call.

*

Melissa had a methodical nature, and twelve years of being married to Barnby had made her thwartedly aware of it. Now that Barnby was gone, planning and performing filled her days as neatly as though they were jam-pots, and at each day's ending she seemed to have filled another jam-pot, written date and contents on it, and put it by for some queer kind of future consumption. Only the planned-for conversations, in the course of which she was to say that artists don't really want home life, etc., remained unpotted. Though it was too early to perform the overture about living apart, she had a quite warm wish to run through the middle section and made several attempts to get it a hearing; but Sawbridge people were so contented in their narrow cells—there Barnby had been perfectly right— that an 'Oh' or a 'Really?' was all that could be got out of them. As for the unspecified person who had seen Barnby looking uncared-for, there was no vestige of him. But various acquaintances took the trouble to tell her they had read something about him in an evening paper, or had heard that *The Scorpion and the Scales* looked like running for

the next five years. The absence of such people was better
than their company, and cheaper—for the old faithfuls
like Harry Whitehead, who still dropped in, expected
double whiskeys so confidently that they really had to be
offered sherry. Melissa, deserted, drank no alcohol, but
she ate considerably better. She had always enjoyed cooking, and now, with Barnby's allowance based on the cost of
feeding two, she could cook to a much higher standard,
study and cultivate her own likings, and eat whatever she
had cooked in its state of perfection, instead of curdled
because Barnby was late, or half raw because Barnby was
in a hurry. Nevertheless, she remained thrifty. In the early
days of her marriage, thrift had been necessary, for Barnby
was poor and she was honest, resolved to keep out of debt
and look the fishmonger in the face; and though the need
to be so clever and contriving, so skilful with lentils and
sparing with butter and inventive with flavourings, had
diminished as Barnby's free-lancing became less free and
more profitable, the satisfactoriness of these feats persisted, and economical stratagems that had formerly been
part of the day's work took on a quality of art and self-
expression. For thrift was as much in her nature as
method and part of her pleasure, an ingredient in her
gluttony, a condiment in her self-esteem. She ate merit
with every leisurely, solitary, well-contrived meal. At
times, too, she ate Molly and Barnby—especially on cold
wet evenings, when the alternative of dragging out to
some restaurant or eating fudge and omelette at home
would be particularly stark. On these evenings the jam-
pot day was zested, so to speak, with righteous melancholy
and scratched off on the calendar as another day of semi-
widowhood stoically endured, with only this to be said

for it, that it brought her nearer to when Judy came home
for the Christmas holidays.

*

The holidays turned out to be rather a strain and rather
a bore. Judy had outgrown her Sawbridge friends and
could talk of nothing but school, horses, hairdressing, and
a little girl called Tracy. Besides, she had to see her father.
There were three meetings in London—once for the
ballet, twice for the circus. On each occasion, Melissa
felt that she was not really meeting Barnby—only being
in his vicinity and trying to keep out of his grasp, as in
Blind Man's Buff. He was thinner, and looked older;
but since he also looked a great deal spryer, these changes
made Melissa feel at a disadvantage. She fended off his
natural manly inclination to ask how she was getting on
without him till the close of the third meeting. Then, just
as she got into the car to drive home, Judy said she must
go to the Ladies', and Melissa was caught. Barnby, who
had come with them to the car park, got into the front
seat before she could escape after Judy. 'I have been wanting to talk to you,' he said. 'I want to know how you are
really getting on.'

'I think Judy ought to be confirmed,' she replied.

Judy came back from the Ladies', saying that she had
been sick. During the drive to Sawbridge, Melissa had to
stop several times for Judy to be sick again, and though the
telephone was ringing when they entered the house, it was
left to ring, for in cases of food poisoning, as Melissa knew,
the patient must immediately be put to bed with hot-water
bottles.

It rang again, two or three times, but by then she was

waiting for the doctor and had no patience for what was probably Harry Whitehead in pursuit of a drink. The doctor came and diagnosed gastric influenza as infallibly as if he were prescribing it. 'I expect you'll be up all night,' he said to Melissa, pulling on his gloves and snuffing the fog from the doorstep. 'And here's a policeman. Well, Officer, who wants me now?' The policeman, however, did not want Dr. Larpent. He had come round from the police station, where the sergeant had been rung up by Mr. Robinson, who was anxious to know if Mrs. Robinson and the little girl had got back from London.

It was past two in the morning before Melissa bethought herself that, having delivered his message, the policeman had probably done no more. If only from common charity, she ought to ring up Barnby. In the hollow of the night, and in that room so desolately full of shopping bags thrown down anywhere, perhaps she was rather glad to do so. She got the number, and as suddenly as if it had come down the chimney on a broomstick Molly Cullen's voice was beside her.

'Melissa? Now, how good of you to ring. Poor Barnby was frantic with anxiety; he thought Judy might be ill, and then there was no answer on your telephone, so he thought there had been a car accident. The relief, when that angel voice from the police station . . . Barnby, honey, wake up and talk to Melissa.'

Melissa heard the change of breathing and said quickly, 'So you know already?'

'I know you're back,' he said. 'I got that from Sheridan. But what happened? Why were you so long getting down?'

'Judy being sick every five minutes,' she said.

68

'What's wrong with her? I say, Melissa! Have you got Larpent?'

'What? . . . Sorry, Barnby, she's calling me, I must go.'

She put back the receiver and sat for a long time in the speechless house, thinking of Molly and Barnby lying side by side, while those final words lingered and slowly melted in the mouth that had spoken them, flavoured as if with some kind of honey made by hornets.

*

It was not till a week later that Melissa realized the impoliticness of that moment of natural revenge.

Dr. Larpent was again pulling on his gloves and talking himself out of the house. 'Well, that's nicely over. Just keep her in bed for a couple of days longer, and feed her up. She'll be having a visitor tomorrow, I fancy.'

'A visitor?'

'Oh yes, she's quite up to a visitor. Mr. Robinson will be coming in the afternoon for half an hour or so. He's been ringing me up for a medical bulletin every day. You had your hands full; he didn't want to add to your burdens, so it was very natural, very natural. We-ell, well, there we are. Now I must be off to Mrs. Drummond. Ha!'

Barnby and I feel we might be happier if we live apart, etc. She might say it yet, but it would be no news to Sawbridge. Mrs. Drummond, that wonderful nonagenarian, kept alive only by her interest in others, was injected every morning by Dr. Larpent with reviving anecdotes, which every afternoon she retailed to a circle of friends. So I can keep my breath to cool my porridge, Melissa thought. She had nursed Judy single-handed for a week; she was tired—too tired to get worked up about her wrongs. To tell the truth, they had ceased to interest her.

To Judy, Barnby was everything that a father on a twenty-minute visit could be: affectionate, congratulatory, and the bearer of a hamper containing every kind of restorative delicacy and a dozen quarter bottles of champagne. To his wife, he was everything she was more or less used to: evasive, surly, cantankerously propitiating. 'And let there be no misunderstanding,' he said as they went downstairs. 'All the things I have brought have been passed by Larpent as suitable for the child to eat. So for heaven's sake let her eat them, and none of your damned putting by against a rainy day.'

'Did you suppose I'd eat them myself?' Melissa replied. It was the first time that afternoon that she had spoken with spirit, and he looked at her for a moment, as though he were recognizing an old friend or a familiar landmark.

On the morning of Judy's return to school, another hamper from the same illustrious firm was delivered. Nestling on the shavings was a greetings card, heart-shaped, bright pink, and lettered in silver: *To my Wife*. On the back Barnby had scrawled, *A few reviving tidbits which I dare say you'll be the better for*. The contents of this hamper were adjusted to a maturer palate—truffles instead of jellies, a *pâté en croûte* instead of cockscombs, the apricots in brandy—and must have cost as much again. It was all of a piece with that card, she thought, outraged at the thought of all the money Barnby must have spent on these gaudy equivalents of what, with a little agreeable labour, one could make almost as well at home. But, aware that in the course of cooking to please no one but herself she had become a much better cook, she decided that she had earned this little bonus. Eating her way through Barnby's reviving tidbits, she even began to think that when her cupboard was bare she might start buying such things for herself—which, with a little planning, cutting down on the hairdresser, not using the car, and offering Harry Whitehead no alternative to homemade ginger beer, she could quite well afford to do.

She was still thinking of it when another hamper arrived. Two theatre tickets fell out of the cut-paper valentine that was tucked in it, and a note:

> In case you'd like to come to the first night of *O Sophonisba*—not that I suppose you'd want to. But perhaps you will eat and drink to its health, so here is the wherewithal.

The wherewithal outlasted *O Sophonisba*, which got a notice in *The Times* comparing it to Etherege rather than Congreve, flabby praises elsewhere, and only ran for a fortnight. So the final splendour—larks (which Melissa hoped were really sparrows, since the death of a sparrow seemed somehow more in keeping with the economy of the universe) stuffed with grapes, artichoke hearts, and vine leaves—was eaten in the spirit of a funeral baked meat.

Melissa was again crossing off the days before Judy's holidays, but this time with less ardour. What with Barnby's hampers, and the interesting experiments these spurred her to, and, as the daylight lengthened, a general sense of enlargement and free sunlight replacing electricity, she wanted no change of any kind. She was entirely happy. Besides, Judy was clamouring to bring Tracy with

her. Tracy was seeming almost inevitable when Barnby
wrote,

> The joys of Easter cannot be truly felt in suburban
> surroundings, where daffodils are so morbidly large and
> lambs leap not, frigidly remembering what it was like
> being slaughtered in New Zealand. So I shall send you
> and Judy to Lyme Regis for a fortnight. All arrange-
> ments are made, and I will not unmake them.

Tracy scotched; and Judy's entertainment provided for;
and hotel meals to appease Judy's seaside appetite—Melissa
was glad to think that it was no longer her business to
restrain Barnby's extravagances. If he could not afford
this one, no doubt Molly Cullen could. And why should
Molly not bleed a little? If she had acted better, *O Sophonisba* would have run longer.

*

While they were at Lyme Regis, Barnby came for a
weekend, staying at another and less grand hotel. Judy, of
course, had to see her father, but this time Melissa had no
such feelings of Blind Man's Buff. Barnby was being what
she called his nicer self, spring was in the air, and when she
noticed that he was exerting his parental authority to send
Judy off to play and that she herself was positively abetting
him, she relaxed, and found that it was pleasantly regretful,
almost natural, to sit, in peaceful middle age, being kind
to poor Barnby, whose play had been such a sad failure.

'But of course you have other plans?'

'Melissa, you have put your finger on it. I have.'

It was the last evening. As the dusk gathered and the
beach emptied, the striped pink and grey ripples came with

a slower, more emphatic voice to shore. Barnby moved a
little closer to Melissa, and Melissa realized it would not
do to make any more inquiries about his plans. Unfortunately, she could not immediately think of anything
else to say.

'I have one plan in particular.'

'Look! Do you think that's a guillemot?'

'No. I'm afraid it's just an Episcopal Dove, hovering
round to abet Judy's confirmation. But we will not go
into that now. Melissa, do you happen to remember the
date?'

'The seventeenth of April.'

'Correct. One month overdue already. An experimental
six months was what I said at the time, which was seven
months ago. As you seem to have gathered, my plan is
post-experimental. In other words, I think I am through
with it.'

'But you love Molly!'

'No. Perhaps I am still rather in love with her, but love
her I do not. It is not in the power of mortal to encompass
loving any woman so incessantly, inexorably lovable as
Molly. I have eaten roses, roses, roses, till I am sick of
them. Simple Neddy that I am, I think I want to come
back to my natural diet of thistles.'

Melissa said with dry lips, 'What about Molly's
feelings?'

Barnby sighed and got up.

'I see you don't like my plan. But you might think it
over.' Barnby could not help talking just like his plays,
where in moments of emotion the dialogue became so
tailor-made that it appeared to clothe nothing but dummies.
But however he had presented his plan, with eloquence,

with touching tongue-tied incompetence, she would not have liked it. As for thinking it over, she had no need to. If a soup is too salty, one knows it without thinking it over. It is only when you cannot throw the stuff away that thought is required; then you think if some potato flour or a spoonful of brown sugar or a violent recourse to curry powder will smuggle it into tolerability. Adjust the flavouring, as cookery recipes say. But Melissa's new life—an orderly existence in the shade of a domestic tragedy, the unharassed pursuit of a sensual ideal, no responsibilities and a reasonable hope of more hampers—needed no adjustments to its flavouring; and to have Barnby thrown into this calm blend, like some cheap corrosive chutney, was not a matter for thought. She did not like his plan. She would not have it.

Unfortunately, it would not be as simple as that. When it came to a show-down with Barnby, he always prevailed. Just as she had not been able to keep him when he wanted to go away, she would not be able to fend him off when he wanted to come back. Unless . . . Suddenly, she saw what she must do.

So, when Judy had acclaimed Tracy with a yell that rang out above every other sound in Waterloo Station, and had been added to the flock of her schoolfellows travelling in the charge of Miss Oliphant, the Under Matron, and had lost her handbag and found it, and had been reminded to say goodbye to her mother and had done so, and had dropped a box of chocolates and picked most of them up, and had been borne away on the two-fifteen, Melissa, with a feeling that she was about to set forth on a tightrope, went to a telephone booth and dialled Molly Cullen's number. So far, so good. The answering voice was the voice that had answered her at two in the morning from Barnby's sleeping side.

'This is Melissa Robinson. I know how busy you are, but can I possibly see you, alone, even for five minutes?'

'But I'd be delighted. Any time, anywhere. Just let me see. Thursday . . . Inigo, massage, poor horses . . . Friday . . . Saturday— Oh, hopeless! Look, can you possibly make it today? . . . No, really? Well, then, if you could conceivably get here about five, and won't be driven mad by skipping ropes—I'm getting my weight down for a teen-age visionary you could pull through a halo—what could be nicer? Bliss!'

*

One never foresees the giant obstacle in one's path, for the very reason that it is as plain, as central, as personal, as the nose on one's face. Melissa had allowed for Molly Cullen being evasive, standoffish, furious, suspicious, incredulous, insulting. She had allowed for her being sentimental and even inconveniently magnanimous. What she had not allowed for was Molly Cullen's overweening self-importance. The woman was a monster of egoism; she thought of nothing but herself.

'Tea with milk, tea with lemon? I think it's so sweet of you to come. Just eat ahead, won't you, while I do a few more bends. What one undergoes! But when I've thinned down to it, it's going to be a marvellous part. The longer I live, the more I adore doing young girls. One can put so much more into them. It takes years of experience to get inside a young girl. Down—and—swing! Down—and—swing! And then critics say how spontaneous one is.'

'I'm afraid I'm interrupting you.'

'This one is just a perfectly ordinary little slavey, but with this terrific vocation, you see—Belgian—and when she goes off in her visions, I see her going all Gothic, long and thin and stiff. So if I'm to do myself justice, I must lose at least six pounds. And now, if you don't mind moving back a bit, just to be on the safe side, I'll skip. I suppose I really am quite crazily conscientious in my work. Always have been. Do go on eating! And meanwhile, tell me all about it. I shall be quite detached from my skipping, you know. One learns that, on the stage. On with the motley!'

'I came to talk about Barnby.'

'Do go on! Seven, eight, nine . . . Really, it's quite soothing. Like knitting. Though why anyone thinks knitting soothing . . . twelve, thirteen . . . I shall never forget what I went through as a fireside mouse and my producer said I must knit a sock. The wool! Fortunately, it soon came off.'

'I suppose it seems rather unusual.'

'Unusual? Not a bit. I'm always doing it. When an author can't think of anything else, he always slams in a heart-to-heart between two females. Do have one of those sandwiches!'

'But I am dreadfully worried about Barnby. He's very, very unhappy.'

'Poor pet, yes. Positive *guignon*, isn't it? Specially about *The Scorpion*. Even though Sophie flopped, we did think Scorpy would run for months longer. But please don't feel worried. It's sweet of you to be so sympathetic, but really you needn't. If I worried every time a play came to grief, I wouldn't be skipping off pounds and pounds now. It's just that Barnby's new to it.'

'He came down to Lyme Regis to see Judy. I've never known him so unhappy. He was almost in despair.'

'Well, he needn't be. It's just the usual ups and downs, and anyhow he carried none of the responsibility, he just writes the things. And this new one's bound to be a hit; it's all mystical and pro-Goddy, and he'll get his royalties as the translator. In the last act, I rush on with a vacuum cleaner and break up a Black Mass. I must admit, the vacuum cleaner rather stifled me at first, but now I adore it. I come on with my eyes shut, pushing it relentlessly in front of me, like a sleepwalking steam-roller. So please don't worry. Try one of those dull-looking objects, they're stuffed with *marrons glacés*. I daren't look at them, they're so fatally fattening. You see, Barnby hasn't got theatre in his blood.'

'It's nothing to do with the theatre.'

'Nothing to do with the theatre?' Molly left off skipping.

'It's to do with you.'

So suddenly stationary, her bosom rising and falling, her legs rather far apart, Molly Cullen seemed to have grown immensely taller and more solid.

'With me? Poor funny me? Well!' she exclaimed furiously. 'I suppose he can say so for himself.'

'I don't think he can. He feels it too deeply. He thinks you've grown tired of him. He thinks he'll lose you. That's why he's so worried. That's why I came. Just to beg and implore you. Don't be unkind to Barnby! Don't ruin his whole life. You mean everything to him, everything! Don't break his heart!'

Molly Cullen had really listened. Now her silence was like the first unpenning of applause that tells the tightrope walker that his feat is over, that now all he has to do is to slide gracefully down the further support. Overcome with relief, Melissa burst into genuine hideous tears.

'There, there, cry away, Mrs. Robinson! You're an angel, you're a heroine. Talk about *La Dame aux Camélias*. . . . I feel ready to cry myself. Here's a handkerchief.'

Forgetful of her art, Molly Cullen devoured three of the dull-looking cakes, and continued to pat Melissa.

'Don't worry another moment about your Barnby. He's not fit to black your boots, but I'll make a king of him. I swear it. I'll be so sweet to him he won't know himself.'

'You really promise? He's got a queer temper, but you're his whole life. You won't let him drift away, just because of a misunderstanding?'

'I promise.'

'For you love him, don't you? And you won't say a word about this afternoon, will you?'

'Not a word. It will be our secret.'

'Our secret.'

'Our secret. And our Barnby.'

Molly Cullen's experience in bringing down the curtain ended their interview on this traditionally lofty note. Indeed, it was time. There was nothing more to say, and very little left to eat.

*

Three months later, after a coroner's court had pronounced a verdict of accidental death on Barnby Robinson, the author of several brilliant comedies, whose adaptation of *La Bonne à Tout Faire*, with Miss Cullen in the title role of Mary Martha Maria, was the success of the year, they might have met again, and on an equally lofty and traditional note; but shock sustained during the accident by which Mr. Robinson met his death prevented Miss Cullen from attending the funeral. Mrs. Drummond, still kept alive by her interest in others, knew all about it from a great-niece whose husband had met a man who saw the accident. No accident at all, piped Mrs. Drummond. One moment, Barnby was sitting beside her, and a moment later he opened the passenger door and jumped out; and of course, as the woman was driving much too fast, he broke his neck. Women should not be allowed to drive.

Harry Whitehead, who was Barnby's executor, accompanied Melissa to the funeral—where, to her surprise, a number of people whose attendance would afterward be recorded in the press, recognized him with great cordiality —and went home with her afterwards. They had sherry and biscuits, and she opened a jar of stuffed olives for him. It was the least she could do. Harry explained that Melissa was the sole legatee—'and as far as I can see, it won't work out too badly for you and Judy. Barnby was level-headed enough where investments were concerned.'

'I'm not afraid of poverty,' she replied.

This was true. It was not poverty she dreaded but the divorce from luxury. In those insipid unhampered years ahead, the triumphs of thrift might have supplied a whet to living—though not so poignantly as the triumphs of expenditure, since triumphs of thrift can fulfil but cannot surprise, whereas she never knew beforehand what Barnby would send next. But thrift, to be fully enjoyable, must be sauced by poverty, and because of Barnby's equally unforeseen investments she was not to be poor—just impoverished. Limbo, she said to herself; I shall live in Limbo. . . . Though she had recollected the word, she was not altogether sure of its sense—only that it meant a place of dullness and vain yearning, probably rather like The Priscilla Café. For ten days Melissa remained a dweller in Limbo and even at intervals in The Priscilla Café, for such was her state of *accidia* that she took to having lunch there to avoid the trouble of cooking. When another hamper arrived, looking exactly like all the others, she began to wonder if Barnby had really died after all, while at the same time thinking he must have ordered it before his death, in which case it might be a charge on the estate. But inside was a card on which was written, *Remembering—Molly*.

Melissa wrote a simple, womanly letter of thanks, and in due course further hampers followed. When they continued to arrive after Molly had gone to play in *Mary Martha Maria* on Broadway, Melissa realized that she had become a standing order.

IN A SHAKEN HOUSE

A T intervals, a subterranean rumble approached, swelled
to a roar, died away. The floor shook, the windows rattled,
the glass dome over the clock whiningly vibrated, the
curtains sidled as though an invisible hand had twitched
them. Directly below No. 27 Ulster Crescent, where Miss
Miriam Turner had come to inspect a furnished bed-
sitting room and kitchenette, ran the Metropolitan and
District line. 'Nobody even notices the trains after the
first week,' averred Mrs. Palmer, the owner of the house,
though the recollection that three lodgers in a twelvemonth had moved elsewhere because the noise was
too much for them made her the readier to 'meet'
Miss Turner over the rent. Having met, it seemed
a few moments later that the two ladies must immediately part. Holding Miss Turner's card at arm's length
as though perspective might enable her to take a broader
view of it, Mrs. Palmer continued to shake her head.
'Not that *I* object in any way, you understand. I'm interested in that sort of thing, I'm a bit psychic myself. But
a professional card on the front door, even though it's the
top bell and could be urged as less conspicuous—that's
something we've never had before, and I don't know
how my other lodgers would take it. We've never had
anything but private cards, you see. In fact, it's quite a
feature.'

She fell silent. She had chosen a bad moment to do so,
for another train was approaching. When it had gone by,

having done its worst, Miss Turner asked if the noise was always as bad as this.

'Oh, no! Oh dear, no! It's because of the rush hour.'

Seeing that Miss Turner was now studying the cracks in the ceiling, and aware that very soon another train would approach from the opposite direction, Mrs. Palmer read the card aloud. ' "Madame Miriam Turner, Palmiste and Graphologist." I'm sure I don't know. Besides, there's the police. What about them?'

Ostentatiously raising her voice as another rumble swelled to a roar, Miriam Turner said, 'I am not a fortune-teller.'

In fact, that was precisely what she was. And, as one cannot practise fortune-telling without considerable insight into what people are thinking and wishing, she knew that if she held out and let the trains do their work, Mrs. Palmer would give way.

*

After several months Miriam Turner was still noticing the trains—or else noticing that she was not noticing them. In a way, this was the more disturbing. To be unconscious of anything so insistent set her on a level with those clients who were so hard pressed by their desires, their fears, their circumstances, that they had ears for nothing but her words and the portentous silences in between. Such clients were almost invariably single women and no longer young. Miriam Turner was a single woman and in her fifties. But, of course, there was no real similarity. The clients did not notice the trains, because something more urgent was clamouring in their minds. When she did not notice the trains, it was because she was growing used to them. And when other clients, less at the mercy of their feelings, commented on the noise and wondered how she could concentrate on what she was doing, she replied, 'But I don't even notice it,' in a voice which implied that she was above being distracted by anything so trivial. Though it was important to preserve this aura of otherworldliness, her outlook was, in the main, honest and mercantile. People wanted their money's worth, whether in the form of entertainment, excitement, solace, a whiff of the Devil, or plain straightforward flattery; and having found out how they liked it, she did her best to supply it. Even when they came to amuse themselves by catching her out and seeing through her, she would give them a good run for their money. But with those who wept and trembled and besought, and insatiably demanded assurance, and stayed for hours pouring out their troubles and their cravings and their disgraceful rancours—for many were more avid to be told of ill fortune awaiting others than of good fortune awaiting themselves—the process was sometimes oddly reversed, and the good run given to Miriam. In mid-course of guessing what they wished her to supply and supplying it, she would be swept on into a further region that was neither supply nor extemporization but instead a kind of idiot infallibility, so that she seemed to be reading off their tense faces sentences in a language unknown to her, and only realizing how applicable they were by the acceptance with which they were heard. That was how she had first begun—or, as she phrased it in grander moments, had first discovered her gift—sitting in a stiflingly hot tent at the church bazaar; for the usual fortune-teller failed at the last moment, and Miriam Turner, newly an ardent member of the congregation of

S. Simon and S. Jude, had volunteered to replace her. Swathed in bright-coloured scarves and not wearing her spectacles, she had gazed into a bowl of violet ink and let herself go, supplying in the generosity of success not only thrilling futures but spells, charms, and incantations. A queue gathered outside the tent, and no less than three pounds seven and sixpence crossed her hand in silver—a testimony that heightened the disapproval of the Turners, who were Chapel by adherence and rationalist by persuasion. 'We shall never hear the last of this,' said Leonard, her half brother. 'Madame Zillah, indeed! As if anyone would take you for a Madame Zillah with Father's nose all over your face.' Leonard was right. Whether it was the rector who betrayed her or the late Mr. Turner's nose, the church-bazaar gypsy was soon identified as Miriam and her stepmother's house invaded by strangers clamouring for more spells, since the green ribbon tied to the currant bush had proved so efficacious, or for further light on the future, since a lady from the East and wearing a sari had come in the very day after the new moon and bought an upright piano. A reporter who trapped Mrs. Turner on her doorstep got short shrift. Nevertheless, a totally misleading account of the interview came out in the evening paper under the heading 'HOW IT FEELS TO MOTHER A SPHINX', and this led to such a row royal that, having observed an ostentatious fast on the vigil of SS. Simon and Jude, Miriam left home on their feast—heaping added shame on the name of Turner by going to a local hotel as a chambermaid.

From chambermaid to barmaid, from barmaid to dentist's receptionist, from dentist's receptionist to keeping a second-hand-clothes shop, from that to the post of dresser at a theatre, she went her zigzag course, never foreseeing where she would get to next, and infallibly arriving where, in fleeting contacts, hearts would be opened, tongues loosened, and such subjects as dreams, portents, hares' feet, and the planets come under discussion. Chance or instinct kept her away from professional occultists. When a grateful client (to whom she had supplied, via the planets, racing tips imparted by another client, a bookie who resorted to her in matters of the heart) left her a sum of money that made her semi-independent, Madame Miriam Turner, Palmiste and Graphologist, set up with little more knowledge than Madame Zillah, though with the experience of twenty years' hit-or-miss practice. She knew better now than to discard her spectacles. A grey-haired woman in a woollen cardigan inspires more faith than a seeress in flowing veils. Her only attempt at disguise was to combat her naturally spare physique, since people find it easier to confide in a plump bosom than in a bony one.

Fortunately, starchy foods are cheap.

She picked her first lodgings in the neighbourhood of St. Pancras and King's Cross, having in view the hard-headed businessmen from the Midlands—a very profitable line—who would arrive by those termini. It was also a good neighbourhood for cheap, starchy meals; and as time went on, this advantage outweighed the other. The income that in 1953 had seemed so buoyantly supporting was degraded to a pittance in 1958 by the rise in the cost of living. Television had swept away the clients who came from curiosity or for entertainment. Some of her regulars, hopeful to the last that the future had delightful surprises in store for them, had died. Others had left London, saying that London was no longer what it was. Miriam's following was no longer what it was, either. Like London, it was full of foreigners: West Indians, Spaniards, and Italians with labour permits, or refugees from Eastern Europe. Though her approach to the refugees was faithfully correct; though she told herself that they were brave, right-minded, unfortunate, and that it was a mercy they had got away; and though she also told herself that all were fish who came to her net, she never felt easy with them. They daunted her—they, or a sense of their misfortunes. Mutely, they held out a thin palm or a letter in a strange language. Mistrustfully, they watched her, staring as if they would pluck the lie from her mouth before she had spoken it; and as soon as she spoke, they hardened their faces as if whatever she might say would be an insult or a denial.

Yet in almost all of them she sensed a gaping, cavernous credulity that went beyond any she had encountered before, even in the most desperately love-lorn, even in the most desperately hate-ridden. If it could have broken through their rigid mistrust, it might have set free in her the gift that had declared itself at the church bazaar; and then they would have believed her—even if they had only understood one word in ten, their belief would have rushed to meet her. But they kept it penned up like a wild beast, and sat waiting to see how little she could do. Speaking slowly and distinctly and in simple language, she told them that a handwriting showed determination, honesty, a love of music, or that the lines in the hand told of sorrows and dangers in the past, many partings, many journeys—but that a further journey, a journey across an ocean, would bring prosperity and an unlooked-for happiness. Her words vanished into their expectation like straws into a furnace. They paid her, and went away. Some of them implacably came again and again.

She began to sleep badly. She grew thinner; omens pressed themselves upon her attention. She told herself that she was getting imaginative. She bought a budgerigar for company. Like an omen, it died. She bought a flower-pot to bury it in, and a miniature rose to plant above it. The rose drooped, and shed its leaves. She thought she would try going to church—it was a long time since she had been in a church. As she entered, her glance was attracted to a painted window. On a scroll below the figure of a young man seated dejectedly under a small palm tree were the words 'I will arise and go to my Father'. That was it! Leonard! Leonard's common sense, his good, plain, pudding character, was what she needed. She would arise and go to Leonard—for a week or ten days. She did not think she could endure him for longer than that. She spent the rest of the service composing the letter that convention demanded should be addressed to Leonard's Olwen, the young woman with a placid disposition and serviceable legs whom Leonard had married rather late in life. It was a letter that demanded composition, as she had not been near them since they moved out to Rickmansworth ten years back, and at no time had been asked to spend a night under their roof. But by availing herself of former days, the increasing force of family ties as one grew older, often having thought of it before but not implementing the thought because of Olwen's hands being so full with the twins, and a well-placed final admission of sometimes feeling rather lonely and knowing what country air would do, she got the letter settled in her mind before the Blessing and wrote it that same evening. Only after she had dropped it in the pillar box did she remember that Leonard's household included her stepmother. Certainly not longer than a week. Fortunately, she had written 'Love to all', which would cover the old hag. Besides, by now she probably lay down a good deal; Olwen's placid disposition would have seen to that.

Leonard's reply, its envelope still intact, was in her hand when the red-haired refugee strolled in, having found the street door open and walked up the stairs. He was one of those who implacably came again and again. 'So your bird, dead,' he remarked. Though he was not the only red-haired man among these sad clients he seemed to her red-haired *par excellence*—perhaps because red hairs covered his hands and bony wrists, so that in certain lights they glittered as though cased in some reddish metal.

With her mind full of an invitation to Rickmansworth, how soon she could get away, whether she should get a new hat, she found it almost impossible to recollect what she had told him last time; but the journey across an ocean —she could rely on that. It was the one thing that never failed, the one assurance they all wanted to hear and accepted, when they heard it, as though it were a due that was being fraudulently withheld from them. 'When?' 'How soon?' To show such a single-minded impatience to get away from the country that had received them was not, to put it mildly, very polite; but, after all, they had not come to England in order to be polite, so why expect it of them? Once again, Miriam foretold a journey across an ocean, and for good measure foresaw him in a large car beside a lake. He paid her and went away.

Her hands trembled so much that she could hardly tear open Leonard's firmly-stuck-down envelope. How extraordinary to be trembling with excitement because of a letter from Leonard. 'I must be in a worse way than I supposed,' she muttered, and began to read it.

'My dear Miriam, I am very sorry . . .' Leonard was sorry to say that a visit just now would not be practical, as Olwen was feeling rather fagged. If Miriam wanted country air, why not go to the sea and get braced properly? That was what he would advise. The intensity of her mortification forced her to admit the truth. She was indeed in a worse way than she supposed. She was afraid, afraid of this red-haired man and of all he stood for.

Her heart pounded, her knees shook. The few yards between her and the door seemed an insuperable distance, but somehow she crossed it and turned the key in the lock. Instead of making her feel safer, this action impaled her on a sense of guilt. The nonconformist conscience of her upbringing, its cutting edge perhaps all the sharper because for so many years there had been no daily use to abrade it, slashed through her defences. She was afraid because she was guilty. Daunted by these wretched beings, by their maladjustment and their unmanageable misfortunes, and disliking them because their misfortunes were unmanageable, she had gone on cheating and exploiting them, taking their wretched money and blithely promising them happy futures—of what? Of being out of sight and out of mind. But what was she to do? With them on her track and now conscience, too, where could she turn, how could she get away? 'There is nothing else for it!' she exclaimed. 'I must give it all up.'

*

There is a germ of comfort in every resolution, if only the

fact of having got it over and survived. Miriam fell asleep picturing the little cottage where she would live on bread and cheese and pick blackberries on a moor. When she woke, the resolution was still there, and half-way to being an accepted fact. She looked at what was so familiar to her waking eyes—the bleached garlands of the wallpaper, the shabby furniture, the Victorian washstand that did duty for a dressing-table. She would not see them much longer. Good riddance, for they were ugly enough. When she had found that cottage, she would have to buy furniture for it—an item she had forgotten about overnight. Could she afford this? Where should she go to find the cottage? It would have to be somewhere remote, or it would not be cheap enough. Yet it must not be too tumble-down; she could not afford repairs. Perhaps it would be better to find lodgings in a little country town. While she lay drowsing, the answer to all her difficulties entered her mind as calmly as sunlight enters a room. Of course. All she needed to do was to move to some other part of London and pursue her profession as before, but with discrimination, never again cheating any of those unhappy refugees. There was no harm in telling the fortunes of British citizens, and they were often made much happier by it.

Some of her clients so methodically looked to her to be made happier that they came on regular days, and if they could not do so wrote asking for a change of appointment. To these she sent notices of her removal to Ulster Crescent; but she left no address at her former lodgings, explaining that she would be travelling about in search of a cottage and expected to find one in Ireland. She also sent her new address to Leonard, expatiating on the peacefulness and leafiness and airiness of the new neighbourhood, telling him that she was already quite a new being, and hoping that Olwen was no longer feeling so fagged.

In spite of still noticing—or sometimes not noticing—the noise of the trains, the sense of living poised above a recurrence of small earthquakes, her vaunt had gradually come true. She had lost many clients by her removal and new ones were slow to come in. But the interest of beginning again, of building up a career anew, gave her an illusion of youthfulness. As Mrs. Palmer said, it was really quite a superior neighbourhood, and with a superior class of residents, since almost all the larger houses had become boarding houses or residential hotels, where elderly people of private means could live in comfort without being worried by the servant problem. It was these elderly people, yawning their heads off in high-ceilinged, cretonne-upholstered lounges, that Miriam had her eye on. In their quieter way, they would be just as good as the hardheaded businessmen arriving from the Midlands; for, however elderly, people never grow tired of hearing about themselves. 'Palmiste and Graphologist' would bring them in. Presently, it was doing so. The line of life, the line of the head, the line of the heart—examining these pink palms, so smooth, so very clean, she fell at times into a professional admiration at the persistence with which the standard pattern was distributed into such a variety of substances and destinies. Etched into those roughened palms that had been mutely held out to her, pencilled on these others like a delicate ornament, the lines, when all was said, were much of a muchness; it was the condition of the hands that told the real story. As for what you said, that was pretty much of a muchness, too, except you varied it to suit. Now, for instance, when she read a journey across an ocean, she put it in the past. 'You have travelled extensively.'

Graphology there was not so much call for. This was a part of the world where people mainly received letters in handwritings too familiar to need any analysis. But here, just as much as anywhere else, she found the clients whom she thought of as 'the real lot'—the famished, the lonely, the insatiably credulous, who hung on her words, who did not notice the trains. These, with their potentiality to release her gift, gave a fillip to an existence that otherwise might have been rather boring.

From time to time, she had nightmares, crude as a film poster, in which there was always a door being broken open and something thrown into the room—a bomb, or a mutilated animal, or a brown-paper parcel with blood oozing from it. Their quality of recurrence made them almost negligible; they were like the noise of the trains clanging their way under the house. Her daily life went on above them, her earnings increased, she made friends with the local shopkeepers. Then, one morning, she had a letter from Leonard. Just like him, she thought, to invite her to Rickmansworth now, when there was no longer any need for it. Leonard, however, proposed coming to see her. He would come next Sunday afternoon.

If it had not been for his clothes, his perpetual, sensible, hard-wearing tweeds, she would scarcely have known him. He was thin, his hair was grey, his face was grey and trenched with lines of worry and misery. He's got cancer, she thought.

'Hullo, Mirrie, old girl. So this is your new place? Good Lord, what's that?'

The rumble swelled to a roar, the floor shook, the windows rattled.

'It's just the trains underneath. The District Line runs right under the house. I never notice it now.'

'Oh well, so long as you don't mind—and it leaves off at midnight, of course. Yes, I should think you've changed for the better. Airier than your last place. Classier, too. How's business?'

'Not too bad.'

'Splendid! And you're looking well. Glad to see that.'

But his gaze, wandering blankly over the room, had not rested on her face. Whatever brought him here, it was not anxiety for her health.

'Clever idea, too, the way the street door opens on its own. That must save you a lot of running up and down stairs.'

And whatever brought him, it was something he was slightly ashamed of, or he would not have been so anxious to wag his tail.

'Yes, I'm glad to find you looking so well. You know, Mirrie, that visit you thought of making us—I was really upset at having to put you off. But as things are, our house is no place for anyone's holiday. I didn't go into it at the time, but——' He took off his muffler, folded it with extreme care, and laid it down beside his hat. 'It's Mother. She's killing us.' There was an evening paper in his pocket. He drew it out, smoothed it, and laid it near the muffler. 'You never liked her, so it will be no surprise to you.'

'No. I never liked her. She was a bit too managing.'

'Managing! You should see her now. Yes, if you want to know what managing is, you should see her now. Day and night, Mirrie, she's at it. Nothing's done but she must do it all over again. When the table's laid for supper, she'll have everything off because it's the wrong cloth. When that's put right, the beetroot will be in the wrong dish, so it must be changed into the right one, and the first dish washed up and put away before anything else; and after that, she'll have to make a new pot of tea because she's sure Olwen forgot to warm the pot beforehand. We've no sooner got to bed than she hears a mouse, or a tap left running, and has us up to deal with it. Or she'll go down at three in the morning, because she's remembered a pillow slip that wanted darning and must turn out the linen cupboard to get at it. Then there's the telephone—I had it put in to save Olwen, because whenever she went out shopping, when she got home she was sure to find Mother moving all the furniture, or rehanging the curtains, or taking down the pictures, or taking up the carpet. Now Mother's for ever ringing up the tradesmen to counterorder things, or to say they're too expensive, or that she's weighed them and they're short weight. And the way she speaks to them! . . . I suppose it's tragic, really. I suppose it's left over from after Father's death, when she worked so hard and managed so well. But what makes it so awful, Mirrie, is how she complains all the time, and tells everyone how she has to do this and do that, and how all the hard work is left to her, and how she's nothing but a slavey in her old age, and works herself to the bone and never gets a word of thanks for it.'

'Poor Olwen!'

'You may well say so. I tell you, Olwen's life is hell. And she's getting worn out. I never come home from work without expecting to find her dead. It's because of Olwen I've come to you.'

So that was why Leonard had looked so propitiating. Miriam stiffened.

'For her sake, and Leslie's. You see, Leslie's old enough now to have her boy friends, and, naturally, she'd like to bring them to the house. But it's impossible, because of the way Mother behaves. You remember how strict she was with you and Kate? None of that now. If a young man comes to the house, the way she talks and nudges and draws his attention to Leslie—it's downright disgusting. She's worse than any madam in a bawdy house.'

'Why can't Kate take her for a bit? She's Kate's mother, too.'

'That's no go—even if Kate would. You see, when I married, she talked so about old horses turned out to die that I promised we'd always keep a place for her.'

He swallowed, and said, staring at the floor, 'Mirrie! You couldn't give me any idea how much longer she'll last?'

Miriam took a step backward. He followed her, as though it were a figure in a dance.

'I suppose you could say that I've changed my tune. And that considering the past it's a bit late to come to you for this sort of thing. Well, perhaps it is. I'll grant it. But I'm desperate.'

She felt as though her will had been dislocated. A moment before, it had seemed plain that Leonard's intention was to hand over some part of his burden, and she had resolved not to give way. Now it was this. Yet instead of relief, only a different refusal was there.

'You do it for others, Mirrie. Won't you do it for me?'

'I don't see how I can, Leonard. It's not that I don't pity you—but fortune-telling's peculiar. One has to do it one's own way. And a person at Rickmansworth isn't the same as a person sitting opposite one. I'd have nothing to go on.'

'I've thought of that. You know how one sometimes reads in the papers when someone's disappeared, how they take something belonging to that person to a medium, to a clairvoyant. And it puts her on the scent. She sees a wood, or a railway station. Well, I've brought Mother's vest.'

He had it in a paper bag, which he took from his pocket. 'Where shall I put it? Here, on this little table?'

'Oh hell, Leonard, what am I to say? I've never done this sort of thing. Yes, put it on the table.'

'And shall I draw the curtains? Would you like me to wait outside?'

'While I burn some dried toads? No, just sit down and keep quiet. Read your evening paper or something, and don't stare at me.'

'Yes, of course. I'll read my paper. Mirrie! Just a moment. Why are you combing your hair?'

'It helps to concentrate. Now settle yourself, and keep out of it.'

She sat down at the little table, and waited for her reluctance to pass before laying her fingers on the vest. It was a woollen vest, with a darn in it—she'd know that darn anywhere; and it had been worn. Leonard must have pinched it from the washing basket. Cautiously, her fingers descended. An old woman's vest. How long would she last? Which would be the first to wear out, the garment or the woman? A smell of aged flesh, mingled with the scent of violet talcum powder, detached itself from the vest. It made the wearer painfully actual, and Miriam

flinched away as though her stepmother's voice had proclaimed, 'It's me.' Intimidated by such vitality of dislike
and so much unwillingness to carry out this grisly performance, Miriam was on the brink of saying she could
not go on. She looked at Leonard. A train was approaching; she saw him clench his teeth, and remembered how,
as a little boy, he used to clench them in just the same way
on the taste of his iron tonic. And that mother still had
her claws in him. No, she must go on with it! She would
go on till the next train, with her fingers on the vest and
the smell in her nostrils. How long would its wearer last?
How long would this smell make part of the world? She
shut her eyes and struggled to make her mind a blank. A
blank it remained.

The next train approached. She relaxed and looked
round. Leonard had put down his paper and was staring
at her with a startled expression. It was as if he had just
seen her in some totally new light. Poor Leonard, brought
at last to believe in her gift and now to be told that it had
no comfort for him. But why should she not say something
comforting? She did to others.

'She won't last much longer,' she said.

The rumble swelled to a roar, the floor shook, the
windows rattled, and the walking stick he had propped
against a chair fell with a clatter. The noise covered their
inability to find decent words with which to close a
disgraceful transaction.

'I'll make some tea,' said Miriam, rolling up the vest.

'No, thank you, I won't stay. I must get back. Miriam,
I can't tell you how grateful I am, what a weight you've
lifted off my mind. Thank God I came!'

'Does Olwen know?'

He shook his head. 'I couldn't tell her—the strain. I don't think I shall tell her.'

'Much wiser not.'

'But you'll come—later on, you'll pay us that visit!'

He put the vest in his pocket; he wound the muffler round his neck. Miriam longed to be rid of him, her gull and her partner in an atrocity.

'Your hat. Your gloves. Your paper.'

'Bless my soul! It went clean out of my head. Mirrie, look at this! I read it while I was waiting, and it was all I could do not to interrupt you there and then. No. 17 Olcott Street. That was your old place, wasn't it?'

WIDOW BATTERED TO DEATH

Early this morning, Mrs. Sheila Underwood, who lives at 17c, Olcott Street, N.W.1, heard cries for help coming from overhead. She woke her husband, and they ran upstairs. The cries had ceased, but they made their way into the flat occupied by Mrs. Flora Gallagher, an elderly widow living alone. Mrs. Gallagher was lying on the floor, bleeding from wounds in the head and face. A red-haired man stood beside her, grasping a coal-hammer. 'I said to him,' relates Mrs. Underwood, ' "You brute, what have you done to her?" He didn't seem to hear me. My husband grabbed hold of him, but he didn't attempt to get away. It didn't seem to occur to him.' The police were summoned, and the man was taken into custody. Mrs. Gallagher died on the way to hospital.

'I'm sure she never injured anyone in her life,' said Mrs. Underwood later. 'She was a dear old lady and her room was spotless. My children knew her as Grannie, and it has upset them no end.' The police have ascertained that the man is Tibor Keszthely, aged thirty-nine, a Hungarian refugee.

'It might just as easily have been you,' said Leonard.

She nodded. The red-haired man—she was safe from him now. An abject thankfulness distilled from her like a sweat. 'Yes. I suppose it might have.'

'My word, I'm glad you left that place when you did. A widow, too, a poor old widow! Makes you wonder what's become of the Ten Commandments. Well, Mirrie, I must be off. I can't thank you enough. No, don't come down with me. I'll see myself out.'

It was to be hoped he wouldn't start putting widows together.

She walked over to the window and threw up the sash. The room certainly needed airing. It stank of lies, and of blood, and of old women, and of disgrace. But it no longer contained fear. No more nightmares would burrow under her days. When she was sixty and could draw her old-age pension, she would retire, she would wash her hands of the whole thing. Till then, she would reflect on her mercies, and never again say anything definite, anything that a hope could be pinned on, that a hope could be shattered on. There went poor Leonard, running away with his booty. He went faster and faster, almost breaking into a trot, so dazzled by the prospect of his mother's death, in such a hurry to get home and look at her in the light of this new knowledge, that he didn't notice where he was going, and collided with a man who was coming up the street. She could see Leonard apologizing, and the man saying nothing. The man came on, walking slowly, and pausing to read the names of the boarding houses, the cards framed in the bell panels. A slow reader—or a man with time to kill. No. 31. No. 30. No. 29. No. 28. Outside No. 27, he seemed to be pausing more attentively. Then he took a step or two backward and stared up at the house, his glance pausing at the first, the second, the third-floor windows, as he had paused before each door. Just when she had recognized him she did not know. All she knew was that in an instant his glance would travel a stage further and that she would be looking down into the face of the red-haired man.

THE OLD NUN

AFTER the unpredictable current of living had swirled her past the point of death and back into life again (and in such an old woman, and one so tired, the Mother Superior's recovery seemed like a miracle to them all) and Dr. Kennedy, saying, 'Well, Madam, you're not dead this time,' had declared her out of danger, her married sister was allowed to visit her for a quarter of an hour. Into the extreme cleanliness and dispassionateness of the room Everina brought a smell of hot pavements, smoke, and car exhaust, as if some part of the industrial Thames-side town had shoved in with her. A large bouquet of white China asters shook with the pulse of her hand; her grey hair stuck out in tufts beneath a hat that was too small and too alert for her broad emotional face, and as she sat down a bus ticket dropped on to the floor.

'Oh, Chrissie, my love, what a scare you've given us! Not that I believed it. I never did. I wasn't going to give in. I just wouldn't believe it.'

'No, dear. You never had much faith, had you?'

'Oh! Oh, you wretch! Well, I can see you're yourself again, biting my head off as usual, the same old catnip— and that's a comfort.' Tweaked back from that imminent fit of weeping, she settled herself more squarely on the bent-wood chair, drew a deep breath as if she were about to say a great deal and instead remained silent, obedient, and smiling.

'Well, Everina. Go on, I can see you're bursting.'

'Chrissie, I am. I've got a piece of news for you, and

thank God you're alive to hear it, for it's good news this time. Poor Ellen's Mary is out of the hospital and walking as well as ever. And that's not all. She's going to be married, and I couldn't like him better if I'd chosen him myself— the house surgeon at the hospital, and he was in love with her from the moment he saw her carried in all over blood on a stretcher. He's called Vincent Jones, he's got five brothers and three sisters, his father's a farmer in Hereford-shire, I've seen all their photographs, and they've written the nicest letters. Such a good steady young man! Even Ellen's pleased, and she's coming out of black for the wedding. In October, and then he's going to a practice in Cumberland, the Lake district, think how romantic! Will you ever forget that evening we went in a boat on Ulls-water? And, Chrissie, best of all, there's a house with it, so she can have all the children she wants without disobliging anyone. Five bridesmaids, no less. Three of ours and two of his. I've tacked up our three's already—taffeta, the colour of Petit-Beurre biscuits, with brown velvet muffs. Chrissie, I'm just beginning to feel I can enjoy it! It hasn't really seemed true till now—now, when I've seen with my own eyes that you're not dying. That's the worst of being my age—your heart's all over the place so!'

To the woman listening, it seemed true enough for her to ask, 'And what's happening about Ellen?'

'Ellen? Well, she's coming to me. After all, she's my own daughter-in-law, and she can't be left alone with poor Billy. I'm really looking forward to Billy; it's nice to think there's one grandchild who'll never be anything but a baby.'

'If you've no great talent for faith, you'll make up for it with charity. Now tell me about yourself.'

'Me? There's nothing to tell about me. Or do you mean what shall I wear for the wedding? Do you think it would be positively indecent if I wore pink? I do so adore pink, and I shall never get another chance.'

*

When Everina was gone—taken out after exactly fifteen minutes, as if she were some precise feat in cookery—though the room resumed its stillness, the stillness was not of the same quality. Listening had brought sounds into it— the creaking of the chair that had been so excitedly sat on, the hooting of the tugs on the river. There had been a night when she thought the tugs were trying to get her away, but try as they might, poor dutiful creatures, they could not budge her, for the weight of her limbs pinned her to the bed. And so Mary, God bless the child, was going to be married in pink. No, not in pink—what nonsense!—but she would go in a boat on Lake Ullswater with a good steady young man whose name was Vincent Jones. It was the sky that would be pink, the evening sky; and as the sunset faded, and the westward hills darkened and put on cloaks of contourless velvet, and every stroke of the oars cut a deeper swathe of darkness, and the ripples smacked with louder, lonelier exclamations against indistincter banks, the brows of the eastward fells would be clear and detailed in a hoary light, like moonlight, or like a powder-ing of frost. But it *was* moonlight, and the music had come with it, dance music sounding in the hollow shell of the tall hillsides; and now, as the boat rounded the bend, she could see, behind the silhouette of the oarsman, the lighted windows of the house on the shore, streaming with light, and flung open so that the music could be heard far and wide, calling impatiently for the dancers to come to it. So now she must stand up in the boat and dress herself in her ball dress. But which? The boat was full of them, a cargo of ball dresses, for she had not been able to decide among them before she set out, so she had brought them all with her. It was really rather silly to be standing up in a silk petticoat, bare-necked and bare-armed on such a chilly evening, dressing oneself on a boat in the middle of Lake Ullswater, and all because one had not been able to make up one's mind what to wear. Here was a dress that would do very nicely. It was made of white lace, and the scarf that matched it was sewn with milk-white sequins in a pattern of little Japanese fish. But in a ballroom one white dress is very much like another, and this dress hooked up at the back, a difficult dress to get into standing in a small rowing boat, so the yellow dress that was narrowly pleated like Greek statuary would be better, if she could find the scarlet sandals that went with it. When she had found the sandals under the bilge board, they were sopping wet; but here was a charming pair of grey slippers, quite dry, and warm, too, being lined with grey swansdown. Yes, that was it, and the dress had grey swansdown round the bosom and was the changing colour of blue-grey hydrangeas. She was half-way into it, and the trombones in the band were heavily breathing out the strong beat of a waltz measure, saying, '*Coom,* *Coom,*' in their Cumberland accents, when she remembered that the dress she wanted to wear was the dress of pink tinsel. But when she picked it up from the floor of the boat where it lay glimmering and pale as the drowned Ophelia it turned itself into a dress of green velvet that had never belonged to her, wouldn't fit her, and had a most inconvenient fan fastened to it, that clattered like a Venetian blind. How tiresome it was to have so many dresses, and to be obliged to decide among them! And the lighted house was now so near (for the boatman, whose beard flowed down his waistcoat like a waterfall, was rowing faster and faster) that she could see the polished empty floor and the trombone's gigantic shadow shooting back and forth across it. If only there were not so many dresses, if only each had not some small thing wrong with it, if only she could make up her mind! Well, at any rate, here was a pair of long white kid gloves.

She was trembling so violently with cold and fluster that she could scarcely pull them on. She gave a tug; immediately a rent appeared in the floor of the boat, and the boatman, growing thin as a waterweed, disappeared through it; but not before he had handed her a packet of starch. . . . She opened her eyes and saw her old woman's hands, that not even a month's idleness had been able to blanch or supple. Practised in wakings, she observed that there was no change in the light of the room, and that Sister Mary Innocent must have been standing there for quite a minute, long enough for her beads to have left off swinging while she stood looking down in quiet approval on an old woman taking a little nap.

'Yes, I have been asleep. And I'm glad to wake up, too, for I dreamed I was back in the world and obliged to choose what dress I would put on. It was most disagreeable, most unsatisfactory. We take God's mercies too much for granted, my child, but I assure you, we ought to be especially thankful for our habit.'

Safe ashore from her dream, she felt inclined to go into considerably more detail, and proffer the funny side of it as well as the spiritual bouquet. A woman of her age, and who had so recently been nose to nose with the King of Terrors, to be wobbling in a skiff in that skimpy petticoat . . . Lord, what is man, that he boasteth himself? But few things are more unedifying than the girlishness of Superiors, and few would feel this more correctly than Sister Mary Innocent. So she asked if Mrs. Kelly's flowers had been put in the chapel, and if their stalks had been snipped first; both answers being as satisfactory as she had known they would be she then said that her nap had given her quite an appetite, and that she thought she would venture on a poached egg.

RANDOLPH

THE date on the glossy new tear-off calendar was January 1 but from the window behind the writing-table one saw the vaguely smiling sky of a London spring. It was a room on the first floor, square, and rather too high for its floor-space. The folding-doors in the back wall were open, and gave a view of the room behind—once the back drawing-room of a Victorian mansion but now furnished as a bedroom. Both rooms were inhumanly tidy and smelled of moth-powder. Two women came in and began unwrapping the parcels they carried.

'If I put the pot of daffodils here, and the anemones on the table . . . Oh dear, I really ought to have bought another bunch! It's such a large room, flowers are lost in it.'

'It will look different when I've set a light to the fire,' said the older woman, who had taken off her outdoor clothes and was tying on an apron.

The fire blazed up quickly.

'It's going to eat coal, that grate,' said the older woman.

'Yes, I'm afraid so. I expect he'll generally use the electric fire. But a coal fire looks more welcoming. One wants . . .' She broke off. Her voice was charged with melancholy and self-justification.

'Why don't you sit down, madam, and have a cigarette, while I put these things away? There's plenty of time. And the smell of tobacco would make it more homelike.'

'Shall I? O, Emmie, I don't think perhaps I should.'

'Nonsense, madam! Much better be easy and natural about it.'

She marched off with her parcels, emphasizing her air of the old family servant. The younger woman lit a cigarette. As she smoked she stared round the room with a reckoning expression, as though she were making an inventory. Halfway through the cigarette she jumped up and went into the back room, where she opened a wardrobe.

Emmie, on returning, did not see her. Her face instantly became sharp with anxiety, but she had control enough to notice that one of the anemones had fallen out of the vase and to right it.

'Emmie! Come in here.'

'Oh, there you are, madam. I was wondering where you'd got to.'

'Emmie, the suits still look creased although we shook them. We ought to have taken them to be pressed.'

'That's nothing, madam. It will soon work out with wearing. My word, what an array! He's got plenty of clothes to come back to, that's one thing. Just feel this!'

She weighed a fold of heavy overcoat between her fingers.

'Solid wool,' she said, 'solid wool.'

'I know. Former splendours.' The younger woman sighed, a little deliberately, and her lips moved into a thin wistful smile.

'And look at all his shoes, Emmie!'

'Well, they'll be none the worse, anyhow. Soap and leather improve with keeping.'

The younger woman had taken down a suit on its hanger and was examining it at arm's length.

'I don't know why, but somehow it looks old-fashioned. I suppose they are bound to, after all these years.'

'It's not so noticeable for a gentleman. Anyhow, plenty of gentlemen are wearing their old suits.'

Emmie closed the wardrobe doors, saying,

'He'll see a lot of changes, won't he? New buildings, and television masts, and cars parked everywhere you look. Yes, he'll see a lot that's changed.'

'Changes in you and me, Emmie,' the younger woman said.

She had gone back to the fire and now she stared at her reflection in the looking-glass over the mantelpiece, and drew her thin forefinger down the deep wrinkle beside her mouth.

'Come to that, I suppose he is changed too, poor Mr. Randolph. Did you notice a great difference when you saw him, madam? It's been a long time.'

'"Seven years." Seven years! I can hear the judge saying it still. Even now I dream about it. Actually, I thought Randolph had changed very little. He's not so grey as I am. Or so wrinkled.'

'A regular life. Besides, he took after the master, and you after your ma.'

Randolph's sister resumed her anxious scrutiny of the room.

'It doesn't look right, in spite of everything we've done. The rooms aren't much smaller and all the furniture fits in. But it doesn't look the same. I suppose it's natural that he wants it to be like his old place, but it would have been easier, I should have thought, and more helpful, to make a clean break. Still, if he wishes it . . . *There he is!*'

The servant ran to the window. 'No. No, madam! It's a van for next door. Funny idea, wanting to come away alone, too.'

'He wished it,' said the younger woman shortly.

'As for the room looking different,' Emmie resumed, in the manner of one bridging an awkward gap, 'it's tidier, that's why. Look at the mantelshelf, for instance. None of that litter of invitation-cards and letters and telegrams and what-not. That's what it is, madam. Being so tidy, it looks bare. If it were Christmas we could stick some bits of holly about, make it less noticeable. But as it is . . .'

A taxi halted before the house. Emmie swallowed, and said, 'That's him!' At the same moment the younger woman gasped, and exclaimed, 'The calendar! Emmie, we've forgotten to tear off the days!' She was still tearing date-sheets off the block when the door opened and he came in.

'Well, Mary, here I am. Hullo, Emmie! So you've come along too.'

'O, Randolph . . . At last!'

'Welcome home, Mr. Randolph,' said Emmie, with sturdy aplomb. 'What an awkward hour, to be sure. Still, I've cut you some sandwiches. I dare say you'll be glad of them. They'll tide you over between now and lunch.'

'I'd love them,' he said. 'I'm ravenous. What are they, Emmie? *Foie gras*, by any chance?'

'Can't afford that, nowadays. They're paste.'

She produced the plate, as deftly as though she had been keeping it under her apron.

'And you've trimmed them with parsley. Emmie, you are a duck. And you don't look a day older, either.'

'Parsley's still cheap enough,' she said. Her stern face was rosy with pleasure.

Pausing after the first sandwich he looked round for his

sister. She was standing by the window. Her back was turned, her hand clenched and unclenched on the flimsy sheets she had torn off the calendar. Emmie's glance followed the direction of his, and her expression changed to one of dutiful concern.

'Daffodils,' he remarked. His tone was similarly changed to suitability and falseness.

Mary turned, and smiled at him.

'Daffodils!' she repeated. Dropping the crumpled date-sheets into the wastepaper basket she began to stroke the pure-coloured blossoms. 'But only shop ones, I'm afraid.'

'Well, I only saw shop ones in jail. They seemed all right.'

'In . . . Oh, I am so glad you had daffodils.'

'Chapel,' he said briskly. 'And the infirmary. Prison life is not without its humanizing touches, you know.'

As though prison life had taught him to have eyes in the back of his head he became aware of Emmie's disapproving countenance.

'How's Jim?' he asked. 'And Roger, and Caroline?'

'We're all wonderfully well. The children are longing to see you. I almost brought them with me. But I thought . . .' She hesitated.

'Quite right,' he said. 'Still, I'd like to see them some time. Perhaps we could make a party of it. The Zoo, for instance. You can get over most things by means of an elephant.'

'They'd love it. They adore the Zoo. We go every Sunday.'

'Oh. Well, perhaps I might try something that would be more of a novelty. What about that Fun Fair at Battersea? Too vulgar? Well, the Lost Dogs' Home, then. I suppose that's still going. Too harrowing? Well—why not the Law Courts?'

'Take another sandwich, Mr. Randolph,' Emmie interposed. 'And would you prefer tea or pale ale?'

'Pale ale, please.'

Her hand shook as she poured it out, and he laid his own steady hand over hers and patted it.

'So now, Emmie, you are nurse to Roger and Caroline. I hope you are bringing them up as well as you brought up Mary and me.'

Mary said, 'Emmie is my greatest comfort. She has been, always. All through.'

Possibly she had not meant to convey more than her justified reminder that he had not been the only sufferer by his wrong-doing. But the rancour behind the words burned through her plaintive voice like an acid through muslin. He turned, and gave her a bleak stare, and only when she had begun to wilt under it, enquired,

'And what was Emmie's greatest comfort?'

Mary's reply was instant, and this time she did not even trouble to mask her rancour.

'Oh, undoubtedly, the cat. But it got run over.'

'It was such a nice little cat, Mr. Randolph—you'd have loved it. A tom, but it had been altered. It used to sleep in my old tea-cosy, a regular picture! It never grew very large, but it was so sensible, and so clean, and so orderly. Never out after ten at night. Mr. Randolph, why don't you start a little cat here?'

'Here? Yes, I'd love a cat. You must get me one, Emmie.'

'I'll have a look round for a good one,' she said importantly.

'What a brilliant idea,' said Mary. 'Just what you need. I suppose they wouldn't mind.'

He looked up with a prisoner's face. 'They?'

'The landlord, I mean. And the Websters—the care-taker and her husband, you know, down in the basement.'

'I see. Perhaps I had better ask them first.'

'Yes, I think it would be as well, really. It's so important to make a good start.'

'Of course.'

He finished the pale ale, and began to look round the room, as his sister had done, quarter of an hour earlier. The suspicious, inventorying glance enforced a resemblance between them which had not been apparent till then.

'How familiar it all seems, Mary. How kind of you to take so much trouble.'

'My dear, don't talk about trouble. I only hope it won't turn out to be a mistake. For I must say, I still feel you might have been happier somewhere in the country. Living in London isn't what it was. Everyone has grown so hard, so self-centred and calculating. I'm afraid it will be rather a shock to you.'

Not answering, he got up and walked to the fire.

'And here I am in the old looking-glass again,' he said.

It was as though it contained, like an alchemical retort, the crude elements of his future; his grey hairs, the alien familiarity of the room, Mary watching him, Emmie with her back turned, gathering up the sandwiches he had not eaten after all. He ran his finger along the bottom rim of the frame. There was the old crack, where he had used to stick the invitations, the letters, the telephone numbers, the snapshots of his friends and lovers. He saw Mary aim a glance at Emmie, put on a patient face, shrug her shoulders and sigh. Not turning round, he said.

'Well, Mary, I mustn't keep you. It's been delightful seeing you again, and I'm overwhelmed by all the trouble you have taken. But now I expect you want to be off.'

'*Randolph!*'

He saw in the looking-glass Mary doing her dumb-show of slighted affection, Emmie beginning to take off her apron. When she had put on her outdoor clothes she picked up Mary's gloves and bag and handed them to her. Holding the door open for her mistress to pass through she said,

'Now, Mr. Randolph, don't forget to eat your lunch. It's all left ready in the kitchenette. It only needs warming up. And remember to switch off the current. Mustn't waste fuel.'

The broad calm face which had shone above his child-hood shone on him now. He shut his desolate eyes against it. And instantly, out of some waste place of the mind, a different Emmie started up and was imprinted on his eye-lids. There was a may-tree in bloom, and beneath it stood Emmie in a grey uniform; but she was slender, and tightly belted, and a man was kissing her. Her head had fallen back under the vehemence of his lips, her straw hat was coming off, her eyes were closed, her face was unrecognizable in its ecstasy. And yet it was Emmie; and somewhere on the margin of this picture was himself, wearing a blue linen suit which the spring grass had stained with its green ichor. Just as the rim of a shiny toy drum appeared, the picture, bright as a soap bubble, snapped, and was gone.

He would never recapture it. So he opened his eyes, and released himself from the mirror, and sat down on the arm of a chair. At some distant date Emmie must have had a young man. And that was natural enough—but why had she not married him? Emmie had had a disappointment, that was it; he could remember fragments of conversation overhead later, much later, for by then he was a schoolboy and not paying much attention to Emmie. Emmie's young man had turned out badly, he had committed some crime or other and gone to prison. Emmie had waited for him, but that was all. He had not come back to her, he had never written. Prison had changed his ideas.

I hope—I am confident—that you will leave here a changed man.

This recollection of the prison chaplain's words called up the image of the man, his exasperated face betraying his total lack of confidence. Randolph laughed. Determining to be in better spirits, he began to walk round his flat, examining the surroundings of a free man. Everything he could need had been provided; food, cigarettes, a bottle of sherry—poor old Jim was still faithful to Empire wines— shoe-polish, a cake of scented soap—the thing above all else that the returning prisoner craves for, as every one knows—writing paper, a copy of the *Daily Telegraph*; even cash. For under the *Daily Telegraph* was a mute anonymous wad of ten-pound notes, secured in a rubber band. Poor odious Mary had done her best, and he had been vilely ungrateful to her. Later on, he would ring up to thank her, and try to be more tolerable. No! Not everything he could need had been provided. There was no telephone. Though he had evaded that prudent intention of burying him in some quiet little place in the country, and had got to London—for postally, at any rate, this morose northern suburb was part of London—there was to be no telephone, no incentive to remember old acquaintances and look people up in the directory, no encouragement to give way to momentary rash impulses. Mary had seen to that; and no doubt had said to herself that it would be so much easier for poor Randolph to settle down and write his ill-advised book on prison life if he wasn't being perpetually interrupted by people ringing up. He found he was staring at the tear-off calendar. April 3rd—his first day; how many hours to go before he could tear it off and throw it away? Tedium, stale fury, and nothing but his own heart to feed on—the first day of a life-sentence. With a groan he walked over to the window and looked out. A cliff of meanly respectable houses confronted him, and cars sped along the street, smoothly hurrying to somewhere of more interest. At one end of his view was a church, at the other, a seedy grocer-shop. His eyes narrowed on a target, he breathed more deeply and more quietly. An errand-boy had come out of the shop, and was packing parcels into the carrier of a bicycle; then he mounted with a frisk and rode off on his delivery round. Randolph began to think what he might want in the way of groceries. Perhaps a regular order would be best.

ON LIVING FOR OTHERS

Explaining that he wished to walk home across the fields, Hugh Whiting left his suitcase at the station, to be picked up later in the day.

'Didn't think to see you back so soon,' said the booking-office clerk, who four hours earlier had issued him a return ticket to London and watched him board a local train. 'Hope nothing's wrong, sir.'

'Nothing at all, Parker. I changed my mind. Silly to go to London on a day like this.'

The words made Parker more conscious of the warm air, the blue sky. He strolled to the doorway and watched Mr. Whiting go down the road and turn off into a grassy track, walking with an easy rhythmical stride. The young porter came out to see what Parker was looking at.

'Pretty good for a man of his age,' said Parker, as if he took pride in it.

'Regular old bachelor, isn't he?'

'Bachelor in his way, may be. He was married when he came here first. But she died. He went away for a couple of years, then he came back to Badknocks, and there he's lived ever since.'

The track led to a group of farm buildings, where the footpath branched off through the fields. They were bean-fields, and fields of standing hay. The beans had just come into bloom. The clusters of black-and-white flowers gave out a smell like that of lilies, but with a lighter sweetness. Oboe, Hugh thought, not clarinet. The distinction had

occurred to him many years before, and every summer
recurred. He was a composer—eminent rather than well
known. The course of time that had made him eminent
had also made him somewhat out of date. The reason he
had packed the suitcase and taken the ticket for London
was that on that same afternoon the Ferrabosco Society
was performing a seventeenth-century masque he had
orchestrated for them. A meeting of the Advisory Committee would follow, and afterward he was to dine
and sleep at Adela Turpin's flat, where he would find
Humphrey Dudgeon, whose opera on Hannibal was in
rehearsal for the Aldeburgh Festival. If only he had not
made that silly joke. . . . One should never make jokes on
the telephone; the acoustics aren't right for it. To his
inquiry how a sufficiency of elephants could be got on to
that small stage Adela had replied, 'But it's *opera da camera*,
darling!' Thoughts of this, and of the Advisory Committee,
where Hilda Carpentras would repeat that the 'cello is no
real substitute for the viola da gamba and everyone would
snub old Jones, assailed him even before his local train
reached its first stop. By the time it had got him to the
main-line junction, he had turned from stoicism to oppor-
tunism, telling himself, as he walked up and down the platform, that if he had stayed at home a sense of duty would
have teased him into doing something about Mrs. Pilkington's Mass, a commission he had spent the last six months
in wishing he had never accepted. If the London train had
not been late, presumably he would have got into it. But it
was late. This was the last straw, and he clutched it. He
sent off telegrams of apology, ate some buffet sandwiches,
and when the local train came in, which it did with exact
punctuality, he returned by it. Now he was walking

through the smell of bean flowers, which would not have happened if he had not set out for London. And to-night he would lie down in his four-poster bed with the quickened appreciation of knowing how nearly it had been exchanged for a skimpy divan in Hampstead.

He reached the summit of a gentle rise and looked down, like a returning Ulysses, on the landscape that had been his for so many years. He could see his ilexes but not the house itself. A tune that came to him long ago and had associated itself with this first view of the ilexes resumed its easy hold on him. It wasn't much of a tune, and he had never made anything of it, but at this point of the walk it would come up and link arms with him, as though it had waited to meet him there, and for the rest of the way would accompany him, step for step. He was grateful for its company, for he was wearing his town shoes, and by the time the path brought him into the lane they were hurting his feet. The rope-soled shoes he gardened in lay in the porch and sitting down on his doorstep he changed into them. Then he tried the door. It was locked. Audrey, excellent creature, had finished her cleaning and gone home. He let himself in. Audrey had closed all the windows but left the inner doors open, so that the air should circulate. He saw that everything was just as he'd left it, just as it should be. All he had to do was to go round and open the windows. But first he must get rid of those shoes. He could not put them down on anything in the passage, for there was nothing to put them down on. Julia had said, 'Let us leave the passage just as it was, so that there will always be something to remind us of how we felt when we first walked in.' And the passage had remained just as it was, with the row of pegs, and the wallpaper of gaudy roses on the low ceiling, under which her coffin had been carried out. Holding his shoes he went upstairs and into the bedroom.

A man and a girl were lying asleep on the fourposter bed. The girl was Audrey. She lay on her back with her mouth half open. The man lay sprawled across her, with his head on her breast. Their lovemaking had cast them into so deep a sleep that neither of them stirred. Ugly, and dishevelled, and disquietingly life-size, they had nothing beautiful about them—only a nobility of being completely unaware.

Hugh was half-way down the stairs before he realized that the man's face was known to him. It was the face of the Rural District Council's rodent officer, a stocky young man who from time to time came to the door offering to put down rat poison, and whom he as often turned away. But as he had never before seen him half naked and asleep, the recognition had been delayed. Now his laggard fury exploded. It was the outrage committed against his bed that angered him. His bed, his honourable lonely bed, had been dishonoured, like a Shakespearean bed. And by a rodent officer! If it had been a plain ratcatcher he could have laughed it off, so much are we at the mercy of a word. But a rodent officer had usurped his bed, and he felt ready to roar like Othello.

The flare of rage, with no action to feed on, quivered out, and left him to grope between desolation and embarrassment. With the pleasure of return torn from him, and made an interloper in his own house, he stood there, still clasping the pair of shoes, and could have wept over his disappointment. But if you are an old man, and employ a young woman to scrub your floors with her strong red arms and her willing nature, and go off on a summer's morning and return unlooked for, you have no one but yourself to blame if your return is not what you expected of it.

*

On his desk lay the *Canzona* for contralto and two bassoons, and in the kitchen was the coffee-pot. But there was nothing for it; unfortunate righteous householder that he was, he must creep away like a criminal and leave an untroubled exit for the lovers. Since the shoes could not be left, mutely accusing, at the foot of the stairs, he stepped cautiously into the sitting-room, where they could be concealed under the sofa; and at the same moment, as though he had provoked it, there was a vague languishing sound overhead, a yawn that shaped itself into an endearment—Audrey waking to her rodent officer.

He thrust the shoes under the valance and stole out of the house and down the path, glancing guiltily from side to side. But there was no one in sight, to betray him by bursting into conversation. Still undecided where to shelter himself, he turned down the lane, past the pond and Mr. Duke's barn and the milestone, past all the things he had noticed with temporary leave-taking when the taxi drove him to the station that morning. One thing had become quite certain. He would resign from the Ferrabosco Society. If it had not been for that inept organization he would not now be wandering comfortless, and driven into the embraces of a bramble patch because an approaching car was too wide for the lane. As it passed him, it slowed down. It stopped. A voice said, 'Isn't that you, Mr. Whiting?' A man and a woman got out and bore down on him, the woman saying, 'I knew it was you. I never forget a face. I'm Candida

Pilkington, you remember, and this is my husband. We're touring Suffolk, and we thought we'd call in on you to ask how my Mass is getting along. How lucky to catch you like this.'

'Very lucky,' Hugh said. So it was, in a sense; very lucky for the pair slumbering in his fourposter bed. 'Particularly lucky for me,' he added. 'I'm on my way to the church, and now you will be able to give me a lift.'

He had not the slightest idea what was to be done with them, but at least he could show them the church. They were papists, but that was no reason why they should not conform with the decent customs of England, one of which is church-showing. He must also show them who was master.

So he watched them turning the car, without essaying helpfulness, and when they had finally done so he got in as though he were accustomed to bestowing these little favours.

'Are you having a music festival?' Mrs. Pilkington's manner indicated a matching readiness to bestow little favours. 'I do think it's such a step forward, using your Anglican churches for festivals. Poor things!'

'Ours is a very small church. Turn to the right.'

'All over pews, too, I suppose. Those fatal pews! Now, in Portugal——'

'Take care of that dog! It's deaf. Personally, I'm in favour of pews. People must sit down somewhere.'

The dog was bearing this out. Mr. Pilkington halted, sounded his horn, and then said to himself in a subdued way, 'Silly of me, of course.'

The money was his, as well as the wife, poor wretched man, thought Hugh. 'It's a very old dog,' he went on.

'And being old, it has not much to be interested in except its fleas. So I dare say we shall be here for some time. Tell me about Portugal.'

Portugal and the dog accounted for nearly ten minutes. Ten minutes would seem no time at all to Audrey and her lover. Allowing them, say, another hour for dalliance and fond farewells, and adding a quarter of an hour to that, to keep on the safe side, and subtracting Portugal and the dog, one hour and five minutes must somehow be disposed of before he could invite the Pilkingtons to his house. . . . Stay! Audrey, warmhearted and domesticated, would certainly give the rodent officer tea. Two hours and five minutes. The hour was now three-forty-five. By six he might call Badknocks his own again. . . . But, no, not at all! There was the six-o'clock news broadcast to be reckoned with; the rodent officer would scarcely leave before he had heard the cricket results. Cricket results and fond farewells. . . . Better say six-thirty.

'Harold! Why don't you get out and move that dog? I can see Mr. Whiting is worrying about the time.'

If he had said he was going to the village he could have made something of this. But he had committed himself to the church, and so must do what he could with it. The church had much to offer. They might look through the burial register for Pilkingtons. Or a notice about swine fever in the porch might lead to a visit to Paigle Farm, where Mrs. Duke would give them tea.

*

'Here we are. I don't suppose I shall be long. Perhaps you'd rather wait outside?'

This was mere hopeful foolishness, since he felt assured

that nothing would prevent Mrs. Pilkington from coming into the church in order to animadvert on its deficiencies. There was nothing about swine fever, so he showed them in.

'If I were to be taken into a church blindfolded,' she said, 'I should know from the moment I was inside what form of faith——'

'Nice little church,' interposed Mr. Pilkington.

'So should I,' said Hugh, with blandness.

After a slight pause, Mrs. Pilkington observed, 'I can't see why you shouldn't have a festival here, Mr. Whiting. It's quite large enough. Too large for the congregation, I've no doubt.'

'We might talk about that. But first of all, I've got to measure some organ pipes. Where would you like to sit?'

One should never go out without a piece of string in one's pocket. Hugh never did, and now he furtively tied some knots in it. When he had measured a rank of visible pipes and scribbled on a piece of paper, he called out encouragingly that now he was going on to the diapasons. Secluding himself in the usual organist's den behind the organ case, he spent the next half hour reading *Thirty-Two Voluntaries by Caleb Simper*, a work that he found there. He read with professional attention, coming to the conclusion that Simper missed a lot of opportunities.

Another expedient suggested itself to him.

'Well, that's over,' he said as he emerged from behind the organ case. 'I'm sorry if I kept you waiting, but one can't hurry over these things. Now, since I've got you here, I'll take you up on the tower.'

'Mr. Whiting, before you do that——'

The tower door was locked. 'I expect the key's in the vestry,' he said. 'I won't keep you a moment.'

'—there are one or two little suggestions I'd like to make,' Mrs. Pilkington went on.

She'd like to make suggestions, would she? Disregarding the woman, he hurried into the vestry. A bunch of keys was rather imperfectly concealed behind a fire extinguisher, and probably one or other of them would fit the tower door; but this was of less importance now, since a far fruitfuller and more congenial expedient had met his eye.

He returned, jingling the keys.

'One or two little suggestions, Mr. Whiting,' Mrs. Pilkington repeated.

He began trying the keys.

'About my Mass.'

Her Mass, indeed! The fourth key turned the lock. The opened door disclosed a narrow cascade of steps, with a dead rook lying on one of them.

'Harold has no head for heights,' Mrs. Pilkington said.

Hugh had no stomach for dead rooks, and found he could temper justice with mercy. He locked the door, and waved the Pilkingtons into a pew, and leant against a pillar, looking down on them—which he could do handsomely, since he was both long and lean.

'I am proposing to write this Mass strictly *a capella*, Mrs. Pilkington. It will be for five voices.'

'Why, we've got more than that, I can assure you. Sneckheaton is a very musical neighbourhood and there isn't much our choir won't undertake.'

'Five vocal parts. The number of voices singing a part is more or less immaterial, provided there is a proper balance of tone. I hope your tenors are under control. North Country tenors are apt to be aggressive.'

This was a mistake, for by incensing Mrs. Pilkington's racial loyalty he renewed her determination to make that Mass her own. A sort of solo for Jimmy Rawson, who could have sung in opera only he wouldn't leave his mother, was one of the suggestions she had at heart; another was places where the congregation could join in; another that *Hosannas* should be sung, *pianissimo*, by a small body of trebles in the loft, to bear out the sense of *in excelsis*. 'And what was the last thing? I know it was very important. Harold, what was the last thing? Oh yes, I remember. *Et in unam ecclesiam.* Mr. Whiting, I want that section to be all in unison, and thoroughly emphatic. I want it to stand out, with a real broad, compelling melody; for, as I see it, that's one of the vital spots in the creed, and we can't make too much of it.'

There was this to be said for her suggestions, Whiting thought: they helped to pass the time. By now Audrey might be thinking about tea. He was.

'Well,' he said briskly. 'If you'll come into the vestry I will give you an idea of the music I have in mind—on the harmonium.'

'On a harmonium?.'

'A harmonium.'

'But why can't you play it on the organ? Can't you play the organ?'

'I prefer the harmonium for *a capella*.'

The vestry faced north. It smelled of mice, paraffin, and ink. When Hugh opened the harmonium, a cloud of dispirited dust rose slowly into the air, and when he tried the pedals, a smell of mouldy leather was exhaled. He eyed the stops. Diapason, reed, bourdon, dulciana. He pulled out dulciana, and the knob fell off in his hand. But it was a game old instrument, and came snoring and tottering back to life under the easy rhythmical tread that Mr. Parker had admired earlier that afternoon.

'Are you comfortably settled? Good! Now we'll begin. *Kyrie eleison*.' For the next thirty minutes, he extemporized in the key of G, drawing freely on Caleb Simper for his material, but chastening it. At intervals, he cast them a guiding word, or drew their attention to a canon at the octave. His guiding cry of *Et expecto* was answered by a snore from Mr. Pilkington, who from then on snored as methodically as a ground bass. The harmonium also threw in some touches of its own, not so easily reconciled with strict *a capella* style as Mr. Pilkington's snores; but in the main it answered to the helm. As for Mrs. Pilkington, she stayed mute as a mousetrap.

I wonder what she's hatching, Hugh thought. He also wondered how much longer his ankles would hold out, for the bellows demanded a discreetly adjusted supply of wind, and discretion is a much greater tax on the ankles than fervour.

Wondering about his ankles, and Mrs. Pilkington, and how Audrey and the rodent officer were getting on, he allowed his attention to stray from Caleb Simper and engage itself with Hugh Whiting, whose demands presently became rather engrossing and led him into the mixolydian mode and a five-four measure. Here a passage seemed to him so interesting that he paused to memorize it.

'And is that the end?'

As she spoke, Mr. Pilkington suspended his ground bass.

'That is the end.'

'Oh. You didn't say so.'

He replaced the knob on dulciana and closed the harmonium, giving it, since he couldn't treat it to a bran mash, a grateful pat.

'Well, Mr. Whiting, I'm afraid I've got to be frank. I don't like it.'

'No?'

'No. I feel it lacks sincerity.'

Just so, with the same uninspired acumen, she would have said to the fishmonger, 'That herring's not fresh.' He was on the brink of esteeming her, when she continued, 'Mind you, we'll pay for it.'

'Naturally. One does, when one has commissioned a thing. Shall we go out, and look at tombstones?'

For, after all, he could not esteem her, and he did not suppose that the hypothetical fishmonger would have esteemed her, either. Fishmongers resent bad manners; they are not marble slabs. Discarding the thought that he would get Pilkington's cheque having done uncommonly little to earn it, he began to question him about the tour through Suffolk.

'One thing's disappointed me,' said Pilkington. 'I did hope to see a man-orchis.'

'A man-orchis? Well, if you take the lane that goes off behind the Wesleyan Chapel and follow along it till you come to the second signpost, and turn left, and left again just after a bridge, and on till you come to an old windmill, and get out there, and go through a white gate—'

He broke off. They were now in the churchyard, and beyond the churchyard wall was the rector, hurrying forward with welcoming looks to greet a young man.

'Here you are! I had almost given up hopes of you. Don't apologize, don't apologize! Better late than never.'

The young man he had almost given up hopes of was the rodent officer.

*

The warmth of the sun and the blue of the sky and the blackness of the rector and the smell of the churchyard yews and the ache in his ankles and all the outrages of that interminable afternoon, from his dishonoured bed to Mrs. Pilkington's acumen, together with the residual surliness that accompanies the knowledge that one has been behaving rather disgracefully, all melted, for Hugh, into a harmonious and Amen-like realization that he could now go home. And alone; for Mrs. Pilkington was getting into the car.

'Hurry up, Harold! We really must be getting on.'

'Yes. We really must be getting on,' said Harold. He said it in an undertone, as though addressing only himself, and just as he had said 'Silly of me, of course' after sounding the horn at the deaf dog. No doubt he often addressed himself, not having much expectation that remarks addressed to others would be attended to, except possibly in the confessional. 'Goodbye, Whiting. It's been a very interesting afternoon. Very interesting. I'm afraid we've taken up a great deal of your time.'

'Harold!'

Harold lingered, as though he were waiting for something he knew wouldn't happen, then turned and walked to the gate. How extraordinary, thought Hugh, that those two may have lain together as obliviously as Audrey and the ratcatcher.

'Goodbye, Mr. Whiting,' Mrs. Pilkington said.

'Stop! Stop, I'm coming with you,' Hugh called.

Since Mr. Pilkington was at the wheel, the car stopped. Hugh got in. He said to Mrs. Pilkington, 'Your husband wants to see a man-orchis—*Aceras anthropophora*—and he won't find the place unless I go with him.'

Mr. Pilkington made unerringly for the Wesleyan Chapel, followed the lane behind it, kept on past the first signpost and at the second turned left, and left again after crossing the bridge, and drew up beside the old windmill. There was no need to guide him; the directions were written on his heart. Mrs. Pilkington stayed in the car, remarking that they didn't want her—her acumen again—and that she'd rather sit quietly with a book. They walked for a couple of miles over heathy pasture land, for the most part in silence. Mr. Pilkington appeared to be in a species of trance, and Hugh was tired. When they neared the place where the man-orchises grew, he sat down and left Mr. Pilkington to find them for himself. Mr. Pilkington strayed and gazed and strayed and gazed, and watching him Hugh reflected on the pursuit—so arduous and so haphazard—of other people's pleasure, and how, in the course of that afternoon, quite without volition or design and totally against his preconceived notion of how he would spend it, he had been instrumental in the pleasure of three people, only one of whom it had ever occurred to him to wish to please, and that one with no more than a very moderate and unspecifying impulse to be pleasant, since the utmost he did by way of pleasing Audrey was to praise her for not disturbing his papers, give her presents at Christmas and Easter, and tip her when she had done something that pleased him. Yet she, and that fellow who was even now preparing an excruciating death for some harmless church mice, and Pilkington—where would their rounded pleasures be if chance had not impressed him to drudge and trudge and moil on their behalf? Chance, and weak-mindedness, since he could perfectly well have hidden in his own garden and never met the Pilkingtons at all. Not that his motives had been entirely pure. It was to spare his own feelings as well as to spare Audrey's that he had slunk from the house. It was as much to wipe Mrs. Pilkington's eye as to gladden Mr. Pilkington's heart that he had set out for the man-orchises. But he was not interested in the nature of his motives. A pure motive is a barren theme; no speculation branches from it; it is incapable of contrapuntal development. Indeed, his motives, even though impure, had counted for very little. Fortuity and a resolute illusion of free will had shaped his course, wrenching him away from the rational intention of a quiet afternoon under his own roof and hurling him unprepared into a career of living for others. It was a very disorderly way to live. Yet there were people who made a practice of it; and though they were usually wan and fractious, they got on somehow; they brushed their hair and caught their trains and kept out of Bedlam. No doubt it was largely a matter of technique, of keeping in practice. It must be admitted that in the matter of living for others he was out of practice. He was a selfish dog—a quiet, cleanly, abstemious, and selfish dog. And his legs ached, and midges were biting him, and he wanted to creep back into his kennel.

Pilkington was beside him, saying rather sternly, 'I hope you don't take unreliable people to see them—people who might dig them up.'

'You're the only person I've taken.'

Pilkington flushed with pleasure. I've managed that quite well, thought Hugh—though in fact he had spoken defensively and with no intention to please.

Seeing the man-orchises had conjured up a new Pilkington. All the way back, he held forth about wild flowers—those that are regional, those that are true rarities, those that are escapes, those that are dying out through the actions of man. The war, he said, had done incalculable harm, turning the British flora upside down. He knew a great deal, and was rather boring. Fairies are said to live on nectar and the scent of flowers, and Pilkington was like a fairy who had just had a good meal. His eupepsia swept him over the reunion with Mrs. Pilkington; he quelled her resentment by being so much more aware of his own satisfaction, and in the end she was forced in self-defence to say that she had been enjoying her book, and had seen a weasel.

'Mr. Whiting looks tired,' she remarked.

'Oh dear, I hope not.'

'What he needs is some brandy.' She produced a flask and a cup, stating that one should always take brandy with one, and that she always did. Nothing could render her less unamiable, but it was admirable brandy. Hugh began to feel more like his usual self, and when they assured him that the least they could do was to drive him home, he said that it would be even better if they would first drive to the station, where he had a suitcase waiting to be picked up.

A DRESSMAKER

Madame Cleaver, late of Bond Street. Modiste and Dressmaker. Evening Gowns, Tailor-Mades, etc. Ladies' own materials made up. Re-modelling a Speciality. 29 C, Mill Lane. Dumbridge. By Appointment.

THOUGH these last two words, 'by appointment', suggested something mysteriously grand and official, as though Madame Cleaver had been appointed by Royal Letters Patent *Modiste and Dressmaker* to the ladies of the Lord Lieutenant of the County, they meant in fact that she preferred intending customers to write beforehand—and were generally read as such. As for the Bond Street boast, there was this much truth in it: many years before, she had worked in the sewing-room of a real Bond Street establishment, hemming and felling acres of hand-made underclothes for the trousseaux of country-bred brides, whose mothers went to Langridge & Harmony because their grandmothers had done so. Later, she returned to her native town, where she married a Dumbridge man, a knacker, and bore him two sons. He died, and the business passed to them. The elder married, the younger took a religious turn and went into an Anglican friary. He was her favourite son, and she was more widowed by his departure than by her husband's death. Yet she lived on in her old home, being useful where she had formerly been essential; for though she knew her daughter-in-law wished her away, she could not think how to comply with that wish. One day as she sat turning a grandchild's overcoat it occurred to her that she might be doing much the same work and getting paid for it. She drew out her savings, rented a small flat in the centre of the town, and put her first advertisement in the Dumbridge *Weekly Echo*. Within a week, it had brought her three customers.

To sit undisturbedly at her task, hearing motor horns and the voices of strangers instead of the lowings of wretched animals brought for slaughter, made her feel so stately and competent that she never doubted but that work would come and that she would be equal to it. When she received her first commission for a tailored suit she felt no particular trepidation; and when the suit was finished and the customer went away delighted with the fit and charmed by the little piping that gave such an elegant finish to the lining, she was not particularly elated. By studying the fashion papers and somewhat enlarging a good paper pattern she had managed it, just as by studying the cookery book and taking pains over the flavouring she had managed the far less congenial exploit of making black puddings for her husband. Mrs. Jameson's tailor-made brought three more commissions within a month. It was a pity that they were all for suits. Wool is not a very interesting subject. But after the third suit came a most enjoyable dressing-gown—purple velours with angel sleeves; and the following year, when the Bishop visited Dumbridge for a confirmation, Susie and Moira Jameson, Anne Nobbs, and Dawn Pulliblank were dressed for the occasion by Madame Cleaver. Such dresses, with their pin tucks, their organ pleats, their little touches of hand embroidery, were a real pleasure to make; nor would her skill be wasted on a single appearance before a bishop, since afterward they could be secularized with coloured sashes and scoop-out necks and gone to parties in.

She would have liked to make more dresses for young ladies, dresses that could be dainty, light-hued, silken, and a little fanciful. Unfortunately, the young ladies of Dumbridge preferred to buy what they admired on the improbably ideal contours of the dummies in Wadman's windows, or Sylvester's, or in that new shop on Cornhill called *Au Paradis*—odd that this should be the French for 'paradise', when as a rule words became French by adding an 'e', not lopping one off. Her few youthful customers were poor, or prudent, or both; they wanted a skirt to go with a jumper they'd knitted themselves, old coats refurbished, bargain lengths, never long enough, made up. And though her clientele of matrons had come to include several ladies who required something handsome for a formal occasion and would pay anything in reason for it, they preferred colours that would not show the dirt, and styles that would not create remark. As for those evening-gowns that still haunted her advertisements, in the course of ten years she had not made as many, and of these, five were black, because black does not go out of fashion. But clouds have silver linings; and if Miss Hartley, in black velvet with her real guipure, resembled, try as you might, nothing so much as a first-class railway carriage for royal mourners, she was atoned for by Mrs. Jelks, who twice sang the contralto solos in the Dumbridge and Westpool Choral Society's yearly performance of Handel's *Messiah*—once in shades of heliotrope, once in electric blue. Mary Cleaver attended on both occasions, of which the second was by far the most fulfilling. Like the note of a trumpet, the electric blue dominated the scene, more shimmering than the violins, more imposing than the organ. Bright, and never to be forgotten, was the vision of Mrs. Jelks, her bosom swelling, her skirts unfurling, rising in a torrent of electric blue satin to sing *He Was Despised*. But all this was a long time ago, and would not come again, since Mrs. Jelks was now singing elsewhere. In Ealing, to be exact, for her husband, a bank manager, had been transferred to the Ealing branch.

At first sight, there was no hint of promise about Mrs. Benson. She did not come by appointment. She did not even ring the street bell. Somehow wandering her way upstairs, she knocked. A certain class distinction attaches to those who knock, and Mary Cleaver, busy just then with a gusset, did not open her door immediately. Admitting an unusually tall woman in a whitey-brown mackintosh with a parcel under her arm, she saw that here was a new customer—but, from the look of her, a customer who would want only a remodelling, of which, at the moment, Mary had more than enough.

'Are you Madame Cleaver?'

The voice was low and slightly gruff, the manner grave and unsmiling. They made it evident that if this lady knocked it was with no acknowledgment of social inferiority, and that if all she came for was a remodelling the dressmaker might still feel aggrandized by her coming.

'I want you to make me a dress.'

'For afternoon wear? Certainly, Madam. Pray come in.'

'My name is Benson, by the way. Mrs. Benson.'

It seemed a casual way to introduce a married name.

Mrs. Benson sat down and began to untie the string round her parcel. The sight of her hands startled up an old woe in the dressmaker's heart. When her younger son became a friar, the thought of his poor bare unsheltered feet in sandals had cost her many tears. Mrs. Benson's hands, still parched with last summer's sunshine, with the enlarged joints of those who develop chilblains in the cold months after Christmas, with the unvarnished nails of those who have grown disheartened and let themselves go, reminded her of Reggie's feet.

'I've got the stuff here. Your advertisement said that would be all right.'

'Of course, Madam. Ladies naturally prefer their own choice.'

Probably some sort of lightweight tweed, or a wool jersey. She would need the comfort of wool, poor lady, as she went up and down, to and fro, in a draughty old house with stone floors. Her hands proclaimed such a life —married, maybe, to one of those gentlemen farmers who were making, or not making, ends meet by Jersey cows, battery hens, foreign pigs; a hard life, somewhere away on the downs, far from Dumbridge and civilization. Whatever the material, it must be good of its kind. No cheap draper would use such quantities of the best tissue paper.

The tissue paper rustled to the floor. Mrs. Benson unfolded a silvery-blue brocade, the colour of a winter sea; the colour, too, of her eyes, though until the brocade was unwrapped they had not seemed to be of any colour at all.

'An evening gown, Madam!'

'Do you think there will be enough?'

'Oh, ample, Madam. I don't know when I've seen a lovelier brocade.'

Mary Cleaver went down on her knees to it, as though

before a shrine. Piously revelling in its intact beauty and abundance, she longed to get her scissors into it, to transform it into something really stylish. She brought out her fashion books. Mrs. Benson turned the pages like a polite child, but without the concentration one would expect of a lady making up her mind on the grave matter of an evening gown. When she spoke, it became clear that her mind was already made up. She knew exactly what she wanted. It was as though the dress were already shaped and tacked and she were describing something before her eyes. And though she seemed ignorant of the commonest dressmaking terms, it was impossible to misunderstand her.

'Yes, Madam. I quite see. What one might call a classic. Now, about the trimming? Some silver lace, perhaps, put on in a formal design. Or do you think it should be sequins? Sequins catch the light so gracefully, I always find.'

'I've brought that, too.'

She displayed a shell-pink net, criss-crossed with silver, and a brown net of coarser mesh veiling it.

'Like this. I don't know whether you'd call it a scarf or a drapery. Over the left shoulder—not bunched, though; almost floating. And tied in a large bow with long ends on the right hip.'

'Quite unusual.'

'Yes.'

She took off her raincoat and stood up to be measured. She stood unnaturally erect, as every woman does who is being measured. But in her case, the difference it made was astonishing. Six foot to an inch when she doesn't sag, thought the dressmaker. A minute later, she was thinking that Mrs. Benson's bust was too low, and should have been supported by a firmer bra. It was a curious thing;

she couldn't really account for it. Here she was, with an evening gown, fallen from heaven, as it were, when she had been expecting a remodelling, or at best a light-weight tweed; and instead of feeling thrilled and delighted, instead of warming her fancy at this rich blaze, she was picking on every opportunity to be censorious. This was no frame of mind in which to undertake an evening gown.

The loveliness of the blue brocade mitigated her doubts as soon as she was left alone with it. And when Mrs. Benson came for the final fitting, and stood arrayed before the cheval glass, Mary Cleaver had no doubts at all. The dress was downright beautiful, a picture! Even that queer trimming was justified, clouding Mrs. Benson's shoulder and bosom like a vapour, emphasizing that milk-white skin. If only the poor neglected lady could have left off at the wrists and at the base of the neck! But with such a gown, she would of course be wearing long gloves, and on the occasion for wearing it a facial and a perm would help surprisingly.

'Where would you wish me to send it, Madam?' Mary had a vision of herself entering the Dumbridge Central Post Office with an arrestingly large parcel addressed to Mrs. Benson, The Ritz, Picadilly, London.

'I'll call for it next market day.'

So might a servant girl have replied.

A week later, she called for it, saying, still like a servant girl, that she would pay now—only she paid with a cheque, and a bold strong signature: *Georgina Benson.*

Small-town dressmakers, dentists, chiropodists, hair-dressers—people whose trade lies in individual contacts—practise, from motives of discretion, the secrecy sworn by priests and doctors. Mary Cleaver did not speak of her new client; she did not even mention that she had been making an evening gown. The ambition had been satisfied. The blue evening gown had expanded in her charge like some shining exotic flower; then the flower had been picked, and paid for, and carried away. She would not see it again, and those who saw it would not know it was hers —at least, she supposed not. Mrs. Benson did not seem a particularly acknowledging lady; she was not like Mrs. Jelks. Considerations like these presently accumulated into a slight sense of grievance. Having decided that Mrs. Benson would not come again, the dressmaker found that she was glad of it. It had been too much of a responsibility to handle that expensive brocade, to carry the burden of it unencouraged by any words of appreciation. Her other customers did not think it beneath them to consult her taste, to be guided by her knowledge of what was chic and becoming. With Mrs. Benson, it was more as if a possessed dummy had come to her for clothing, a dummy whose narrow mind knew what it wanted and knew nothing else. Had Mary Cleaver known the word 'arbitrary', she would have used it; as it was, she said to herself, 'Rather too hoity-toity.' And besides, the discrepancy between the shabby lady and the sumptuous apparel shocked her sense of decorum—her sense of decency, even. How could one be sure that Mrs. Benson would have her hair properly permed and tinted and remember to buy new shoes, and to hide those battered hands under kid gloves? When Mrs. Arthur Nobbs, arriving by appointment, asked her opinion as to what would be both suitable and practical for the Nobbs Seniors' golden wedding and afterward for sherry and television gatherings, and was so tractably persuaded to renounce an old-gold taffeta in favour of a neat

floral-patterned crêpe—the compelling factor being that
taffeta cannot stand up to watching television, it rends at
the seams—Mary Cleaver felt as if she had woken up in
her own bed after a nightmare.

The tacking threads were not out of the neat floral
pattern before Mrs. Benson was back again, for another
evening gown. This time it was a satin, mahogany-
coloured. The skirt was to be draped to show a lead-
coloured petticoat, the trimming to consist of a few
lead-coloured bows. Three sets of bows had to be made
before Mrs. Benson was satisfied with them. It was a
cruel gown to make, and would be even crueller to wear.
But it was what Mrs. Benson wanted. She said so, standing
in front of the glass, intent and motionless. It was as if she
would stand there for ever, like a tree in a landscape, like
an effigy of dark marbles in a church. It needed several
recalling fidgets to dislodge her from her dream.

This was in early November. Five months later, she
reappeared, and once more it was an evening gown she
wanted. Winter had done its worst to Mrs. Benson, but
had not tamed her ambition. She brought billows of
glistening white gauze, splashed with vermilion and rose
and lemon yellow, together with a wide ribbon of
mignonette green for a sash—'like an azalea bed', she
remarked. Mary was about to ask if Mrs. Benson was
fond of gardening—many ladies were, and looked the
worse for it—when Mrs. Benson went on, 'And after
this, there is something else I've been thinking about,
something quite different.'

'A spring tailor-made, Madam?' Mrs. Benson's daytime
appearance made this a natural assumption.

'For sad evenings.'

The word 'sad' has secondary meanings. It can be used for cakes that have failed to rise, for overcast weather. Mary supposed that the next dress she would make for Mrs. Benson would be for those dusky, clammy evenings when one almost lights a fire but instead puts on a shawl, and she was glad to think that for once Mrs. Benson was facing realities. Mrs. Benson was doing no such thing. The silk she brought, patterned in arabesques of brown and mulberry and a curious dead slate-blue, was fine as a moth's underwing. Held against the light, it was almost transparent, like a film of dirty water.

'You'll have a slip underneath, of course, Madam. What shade were you thinking of?'

But for once, Mrs. Benson had not got it all planned and settled. She stared at the stuff as people stare at slowly running water, and said nothing.

'It's really quite a problem to know which tint to bring out. Perhaps something quite a contrast . . .'

To aid her decision, since the decision was apparently going to be left to her, Mary Cleaver began to pass the silk through her hands.

'Oh, Madam, look here! I'm afraid it's past making up. It's been left in its folds so long it's quite perished. Look, here's a fray, and here's another. Right across the breadth, you see. I couldn't in honesty undertake it; it would fall to pieces before you'd put it on. What a pity, Madam, what a pity!'

Her concern was professional and genuine, though mixed with some anxiety as to how Mrs. Benson would take this blow.

'So it is. It's been left in its folds too long, just as you say, and now it's perished.'

Her tone of voice was airy, serene, a little singsong; false, because the situation demanded a false detachment from a true misfortune. She's taking it so well, thought the dressmaker, abashed to have been in doubt as to how Mrs. Benson would take it. But the gentry are brought up that way, generations of them, taking snuff one moment and having their heads cut off the next. She stole a respectful glance of compassion at this heroine. Mrs. Benson had repossessed herself of the silk, and with an expression of gleeful malice was poking holes in its ruined web. Mary Cleaver blinked and looked away, and afterwards tried to convince herself that what she had seen was nothing out of the common, and not in the least horrible. But though nothing more upsetting had happened than the natural decay of a curiously patterned silk, and the silk's lady taking it lightly and as a lady should, Mary Cleaver somehow felt, somehow even hoped, that Mrs. Benson would not visit her again. And though they met once more, the meeting was accidental.

*

It was in August of that same year. The holiday season had begun, and the weather had broken. Dumbridge was crowded with holidaymakers, who came up from West-pool in search of something more diverting than its wind-beaten esplanade and sodden bathing tents, and swarmed in and out of the shops, listless, irritable, and impeding as wet wasps. Mary accordingly did her household shopping early in the day, while the pavements were still passable and the produce unfingered. But on this particular afternoon she was overtaken by a craving for cucumber sandwiches. She had edged herself through the clot of people who were sheltering from a thundershower under the greengrocer's awning, she had bought her cucumber and was making her way out, when she heard a sudden fusillade of titters, exclamations, and guffaws.

'Look at her! I ask you! Did you ever see such a scream? Well, of all the sights! Going to the opera, ducks?'

Other voices, further along the street, took up the View Halloo, and a child cried out, 'I don't like her! I don't like her!' and began screaming.

Two nuns came into the shop, one saying to the other, 'We must get whichever's cheapest.' The crowd made way for them, and through the gap thus created Mary caught sight of Mrs. Benson on the opposite side of the street. She was walking slowly along, looking neither to right nor left. There were people on that pavement, too, but they were silent, and shrank back as she passed them. She was bareheaded. She wore her old mackintosh. Below the mackintosh the blue brocade dress hung glittering to the ground and trailed after her.

Mary jostled a nun, elbowed the gapers and jeerers aside, and ran across the street. Old Mr. Bethel, the glovemaker, had come out of his shop and stood wringing his hands. Seeing Mary, his face cleared. 'That's right, you go after her, Mrs. Cleaver! I kept her in my shop as long as I could, hoping that someone would come. You're a good woman, God bless you, you'll know what to do. She's the Honourable Mrs. Benson, poor thing!'

As Mary caught up with her, Mrs. Benson began to walk faster, paying no heed to Mary's breathless civilities.

'What a dreadful day, isn't it, Madam? I don't know when I've seen a worse August. Shocking for the harvest, too. Fortunately, I brought my umbrella. It really doesn't do to go out for a moment without one's umbrella, with the weather so changeable.'

Making conversation with a dry tongue, and attempting to hold the umbrella over a woman so much taller than herself who persisted in ignoring the attempt, Mary bobbed along beside Mrs. Benson. All very well for Mr. Bethel to say she'd know what to do. Knowing is one thing, doing quite another.

'Dear, dear! Another of these puddles! The Town Council lets everything get into such a state, I don't know what we pay rates for, I'm sure.' But Mrs. Benson had set her brogued foot straight into the puddle.

Grieving over Mrs. Benson's hem, Mary forgot Mrs. Benson's head. The umbrella tilted, caught and unloosed a lock of hair. Three holiday girls, looking silly enough themselves, God knows, with transparent showerproofs over their seaside nakedness, tittered. But Mrs. Benson laughed outright, a spontaneous, carefree laugh.

'Now what have you done to me?' she asked, smiling down on Mary's distress.

'Oh, Madam, if you'd come home with me, I could set you to rights in a minute. And if—don't think me impertinent!—if you'd stay for a cup of tea, if you would overlook . . .'

'I should be delighted, I adore going out to tea.'

She had emerged from her madness like the moon from a cloud. Shedding romance and serenity like the moon, she drank three cups of tea and ate all but one of the cucumber sandwiches, talking of the price of vegetables, and the convenience of gas fires, and of Venice, and Madrid, and Brighton. Discovering that Mary had worked for Langridge & Harmony, she told how she used to go there as a little girl accompanying her mother, to sit watching the fitter and wishing for a little black velvet pincushion to bob at her waist.

'Miss Dent. I expect you knew her.'

'Only by name, Madam. I was a sempstress, making underwear.'

'Oh, then no doubt you made all my mother's night-dresses. She was intensely particular.' She glanced down at her draggled blue skirts. 'I'm afraid you won't think that I am intensely particular.'

On the plea of a stitch in time, Mary got Mrs. Benson out of the blue brocade and into a borrowed skirt and pullover. The skirt was too short, the pullover too wide, but the mackintosh covered these defects. Then she accompanied Mrs. Benson to the bus depot, saw her into the bus, and stayed till its departure.

'Goodbye, goodbye! Please ask me again.'

The blue dress had been left hanging on the dummy. On her return, Mary's first impression was of something invincibly beautiful and sumptuous; but in fact it was past praying for, mud-stained and cockled with wet from hem to knee. This much was the day's doing, but not all the ill-usage it had suffered. Mrs. Benson must have walked over heaths in it, and through thickets. Burrs and sharp grasses were embedded in it, strands of silk had been clawed out by brambles, the delicate net was in shreds and tatters, and dry holly leaves had collected in one loop of the bow, as in a last year's bird's nest. She sponged and pressed and mended it as best she could, made sure of the address from Mr. Bethel, and posted it. Mr. Bethel's mood had hardened. He hoped there was no money owing.

No acknowledgement came, and her skirt and pullover were not returned.

*

When the street bell rang and the man on the threshold said, 'Are you Mrs. Cleaver? My name is Benson,' she could only just stop herself from replying, 'Yes, I know.' Some months had gone by, and she was certainly not expecting him, but she knew him instantly, because in the husband she recognized the wife. It was not merely that he was tall and gaunt and weatherbeaten, and spoke with the same mumbling aloofness. There was a deeper, more inflexible likeness, as if through the years of their married life they had been enforcing that look of fatigue and devil-may-care patience on each other. In silence he followed Mary upstairs and into her sitting-room, where the cat gave one glance at him and went out with a blank face, as though he smelled of fever.

'I'm here as my wife's man of business,' he said. 'I know you did some work for her. Does she owe you anything?'

'No, nothing at all. I hope Mrs. Benson is well.'

'She can't have paid you for that last job, I think—a dress that came by post.'

'It only needed a few repairs, and that was settled in advance. Mrs. Benson owes me nothing.'

He pulled out his pocketbook, and cancelled an item in a list.

'I suppose it was because you were cheap.'

'I beg your pardon!'

'I'm sorry. I didn't mean to be rude. But the cheques she made out to you are for very small sums compared to the bills she didn't pay. Well, if you're sure it's all right, I'll be going. Goodbye.'

'I hope Mrs. Benson is well,' she repeated.

He turned back with a movement of his shoulders that was at once exasperated and fatalistically acceptant. 'Mrs. Cleaver, did it never occur to you that my wife was not in her right mind?'

'Oh, no! I never thought of such a thing.'

'Not even—' he broke off, gave her a furious glare, and continued—'not even when you met her trailing through Dumbridge in an evening dress? Yes, I know all about it. I got it out of Bethel. And you were very kind to her, and I am very grateful. But why did nobody tell me?'

As though recognizing the futility of this question, he put on an air of cross-examining composure. 'When did she first come to you?'

'A year ago. Almost to the day.'

'Exactly. By then the others must have been dunning her, so that she was afraid to go back to them. She'd been buying things all over the place—London, Bath, Cheltenham. How was I to guess?' His cross-examining mask had fallen off, and now he was the man in the dock. 'How was I to guess? She always looked so shabby. And when I begged her to get herself something new, something fit to be seen in, she'd put me off with not wasting money. But all the time, she was getting these fantastic fineries.'

'One could see she was used to the best.'

'I never saw her wearing them, but the milkers did, and the farm hands. She used to go out early in the morning and wander for miles. How was I to know? I was at work then, packing mushrooms to go off in the van. If she was late with breakfast, I supposed she'd overslept. I knew nothing till the morning they pulled her out of the river and brought her home dripping in white satin. Couple of days later—Sunday—she went off again, walked over the downs to Epworth, and turned up at the Wesleyan Chapel in a yellow ball dress. But one can't keep one's wife under lock and key.' It was to himself he was talking, reiterating a familiar, hopeless rationalization of his calamity, as an animal in a cage trap turns round and round, unable to remember where it got in, unable to find a way out.

'I had her certified.'

'Oh, no!'

So might a farmer speak of a cow. *I sent her to the knacker.*

Hearing Mary's exclamation, he seemed to catch sight of her. Frowning, and quickly averting his glance, and exaggerating his mumbling aloofness of manner, he said, 'They say she'll recover in time, with rest, and proper meals, and warmth, and all the things she didn't have at home. That's what they hope. Meanwhile, I'm trying to clear things up, deal with the debts, deal with those wretched garments—for she mustn't see them again. They'll make an expensive bonfire. I don't know whether you'd be able to do anything with them. Sell them on commission, you know, or buy them outright. I'd be thankful to get something for them, however little.'

'I'm afraid you are quite mistaken.'

Shock, disapproval, compassion for the woman she had succoured, mortification because that same woman had only resorted to her when she could go nowhere else, injured professional pride, and a belated, violent realization of the horror she had felt at her husband's trade—all these elements, jostled together, exploded in Mary Cleaver's wrath.

'Yes, Mr. Benson, quite mistaken! I am a dressmaker. I have earned my living as a dressmaker for the last twelve years, and this is the first time anyone has insulted me by taking me for an old-clothes woman. Good morning to you!'

The door slammed to behind him. He was out on the landing, in the company of several empty milk bottles. He noticed them sharply, and thought, These people seem to drink a lot of milk. By the time he reached the street he was shaking with rage, while at the same time waves of self-pity swept over him. Such was his state of mind that he had to spend several minutes looking in at the saddler's window. Leather to leather. Leather suffers long, and is tough. He had endured worse things than being stormed at by an elderly dressmaker standing on her dignity.

A SPIRIT RISES

'But why,' said the ageing man to the ageing woman, 'why did your father keep a rocking horse in his study?'

'Was that odder than the carpenter's bench?'

'Yes, decidedly. In fact, I think all schoolmasters should do carpentry for a hobby. It would be a relief to drive something in with a hammer from time to time. But a rocking horse—a large rocking horse. Why?'

'Everything was larger in those days—rooms, rocking horses——'

'The British Empire——'

'Table napkins.'

(She saw once again the long room, running the whole width of the house. At one end was the fireplace, with St. Jerome above it, his bald, studious head eternally bent, his small lion for ever waiting for a word of recognition. At the other end of the room was the carpenter's bench, with its array of tools, and near by it the rocking horse. The rocking horse was a dapple-grey, with tail and flowing mane of silvery horse-hair. The saddle and harness, scuffed with usage, were of crimson leather, and it was mounted on rockers, painted green. And as a child, looking up into its flaring blood-red nostrils, she had always felt an uneasy sense of pity. Surely anything so red must be a representation of pain?)

'I suppose it was rather large.'

'Ten hands from floor level,' he replied.

They had not met for over forty years, and now they

met by chance in a crowded room, introduced to each other as strangers. They talked with a kind of stiff intimacy, like children at a party.

(The room was a half basement, he remembered: dusky, shabby, smelling of books, wood shavings, tobacco, and sometimes glue. Its windows looked out on a steeply rising bank where ferns and irises grew and autumn scattered fallen leaves from a Virginia creeper. The bookshelves lining the walls gave it an additional sombreness, and as there were heaps of books on the floor as well as that demoniacal cat one needed to pick one's steps.)

'Ten hands. An easy leap for Daniel. Do you remember Daniel, curled up on the saddle?'

'Daniel!' he exclaimed. 'I was just trying to remember its name. What an alarming beast!'

'You should have known Jael. Daniel was mutton compared with Jael.'

'Why did he choose such savage cats?'

'Jael chose him. She met him in the street and followed him home. And nothing could dislodge her.'

'I don't wonder. I felt much the same.'

(The man, dead for so many years, now entered the room carrying a large stoneware jar of ink. The cat fastened herself round his leg, intending to climb up him. The jar slipped from his hand. As it hit the floor, the cork flew out, and a fountain of ink spurted up, drenching everything except the cat. This incident she knew only by hearsay, but on the ceiling a corona of spattered ink, like a satanic halo, remained to bear witness.)

'Why are you so circumstantial about the rocking horse's height?'

'I measured it, one day when I was waiting for him. I

believe it was the only time he kept me waiting. Some ass had waylaid him.'

'He didn't suffer asses very gladly.'

'My God, no! No need to tell one of his pupils that.'

(Laying a hand over a title, for instance, he would inquire what the essay was about, adding that though it didn't matter which end of a worm you took hold of, a given theme should be approached with more respect—if only as a formality of thanks to the bestower. Then, sitting beside him, you watched him read on, slowly, carefully, giving his whole mind to it, while you felt increasingly sick as you remembered passages lying ahead—the eloquent, the learned, the judicious passages you had been so pleased with at the time of writing; and finally you went off, walking on air because now and henceforward you would know how to set about it.)

'There has never been anyone like him,' he said.

Their hostess came up.

'Philip, I'm very sorry to drag you away. But Anna says that unless you mean to miss the first act——'

'She's quite right. We must go. Oh dear, now I shall never know about the rocking horse. But it's been extraordinarily nice meeting you like this.'

'It was his nursery rocking horse,' she said, suddenly relenting. 'He kept it to ride on.'

'He rode on it?'

'And read at the same time.'

'Like Shelley. Thank you.'

Till that moment, she had been fobbing him off, teasing a curiosity she had no intention of satisfying, caressing a private malice, honouring an ancient grudge. It had

touched her to meet this grey-haired man who still remembered his teacher with such living piety. But for all
that, he had been one of them, one of those special pupils
who came thronging between her and her birthright, whose
voices rose and fell behind the study door, who learned,
who profited, who demanded, who endeared themselves
by their demands, who were arrayed for the ball while she,
her father's Cinderella, went barefoot like the cobbler's
child in the adage. So why should she admit him to her
patrimony, to a memory which she and she alone possessed?
Then, because in that sad, submissive, 'Now I shall never
know,' he had seemed to be saying farewell to her father
and not to her at all, she relented, sending him away with
a picture in his mind.

But the picture was incomplete. A figure was lacking
from it.

At the date of the picture, she had no consciousness of
those pupils arriving to supplant her. Perhaps they had not
even begun to arrive, for at that time her father was a
young man, a junior master at the foot of the ladder.
Certainly at that time he had more leisure. The sounds of
carpentering ascended through the house; he fitted new
limbs to her wooden dolls and showed her how to bore
holes with a gimlet. He strolled into the garden, snuffing
the sweetbriar or hunting for slugs among the auriculas;
he was chief mourner at many tadpole funerals. When her
mother was out for the afternoon, he would fetch her
down to have tea with him—in summer under the haw-
thorn where you could hear people walking and talking
in the road behind the tall wooden paling, in winter below
St. Jerome, where the fire and the reading lamp changed
the rest of the room into a cave. After tea, she would stay

on till her bedtime, pulling out from the lower shelves
books she couldn't read and methodically replacing them
while he wrote at his desk, a cat dripping from his knee,
or sat on the dapple-grey horse, reading and gently rocking.
Because of the blood-red nostrils, which had a different
reality from the rest of the animal, she was afraid of the
horse. He must have known this, for he never urged her
to ride on it. But one rainy summer afternoon he called
her to him and pulled her up to sit on the saddle-bow before
him. Holding her round the middle with his right hand,
holding a book in his left, he began to read aloud.

> *'Little Ellie sits alone*
> *'Mid the beeches of a meadow,*
> *By a stream-side on the grass,*
> *And the trees are snowing down*
> *Doubles of their leaves in shadow*
> *On her shining hair and face.'*

Nursery rhymes she knew, and hymns, for the cook
sang them; and a godmother had tried to teach her to say
various little poems by rote. This, too, rhymed and ran.
But it was different. A calm steady rain was falling, and
through the open windows came coolness and the smell of
wet grass. The raindrops splashed on the flagged walk at
the foot of the bank, the rockers kept up a gentle thunder
on the wooden floor.

> *And the steed it shall be shod*
> *All in silver, housed in azure,*
> *And the mane shall swim the wind;*
> *And the hoofs along the sod*
> *Shall flash onward and keep measure,*
> *Till the shepherds look behind.*

The rocking horse was keeping measure, the silver rain was falling in order to be silver, everything ran together and was one thing. She relaxed, abandoning her weight to the hard body behind her, leaving her legs to dangle, rubbing her head against her father's shoulder. The grasp tightened round her, the voice went on. Just as the rocking horse kept measure, just as the rain fell in order to be silver, the voice went on in order to be poetry. It was familiar, and made itself unknown. Lulled and held and enchanted, happier than she had ever been before, she knew for certain that presently she was going to weep; but to weep as she had never wept before, to weep in acquiescence and delight and participation in a whole, as the rain fell in acquiescence to the grey skies, as the ferns on the bank spread out their fronds under the rain. She knew, too, that the rocking horse was bearing them towards a sad ending: that Ellie would die, or the knight be killed before he could be shown the swan's nest. But that was not why she would weep.

Down at the convent they had begun to ring their bell. It was a single bell, high-pitched and over-sweet. 'Ting, ting, ting,' it said in a precise, mincing voice. But presently the iterated single strokes began to trail an echo after them, an echo that swelled and vibrated till the syllables of the bell were almost unheard in it and became a rod of sound that pierced one through like a crystalline gimlet. To this tranquil agonizing cry Ellie found the nest gnawed by rats and the wild swan flown. Her tears fell and fell. He made no attempt to check them. After a while, but now not reading from the book, he began again: 'O what can ail thee, Knight-at-arms. . . .'

THE SNOW GUEST

It was a January afternoon and Gilbert had walked to the upper meadow in search of a little recreation. The warmth of coming home for Christmas, the heavy flutter of Christmas celebrations, had gone by, and the ten days that remained before he went back to school stretched dully before him. There would not be even the usual family jaunt to Plymouth; for Soper, the cowman, was in hospital, and the farm could not be left unattended.

'Going to watch the buzzards?' his uncle suggested. He agreed, though in fact he was totally uninterested in buzzards. 'Better keep moving, or you'll get chilled,' his mother added. To that, too, he agreed, though what he had in mind was a granite outcrop at the head of the meadow, where he would sit and smoke a cigarette. He was allowed to smoke, in moderation. He was allowed to do pretty much as he pleased, during the holidays, especially if he did it out of doors. His mother (he generally thought of her as Helen) and Uncle Bill believed that children should grow up free, hardy, and nature-loving. It was what they were themselves, if the working ownership of a small moorland farm constitutes freedom; hardy they certainly were, and so nature-loving that they cleaned out cowsheds, hen-houses, and rabbit-hutches without feeling impatient with the animals which dirtied them. Helen stretched her love of nature into even greater feats of patience, for she collected wool on sheepwalks, washed, carded, and spun it, extracted vegetable dyes, and made dandelion and elderberry wines. Though boring, they were good parents, and he freely admitted it. He thought of them as parents, for they were all the parents he had known. He was born, a posthumous child, under his uncle's roof, and the brother and sister had kept house together ever since. Their family resemblance, the fact that they spoke and glanced and walked in the same way, shared common memories of childhood, had like tastes, opinions, and prejudices, made them seem more parental—as though they were one compound hermaphroditic Parent. This had made his childhood peculiarly secure, but it had also made it trite and unimpassioned. There was no glint of mystery about them, nothing that challenged him, nothing that he could not understand. Already—he was fifteen— he felt himself older than they, a ripened relative who lived with them from kindly and practical motives.

As he mounted through the steep upper meadow—an intake from the surrounding moor—he began to believe that he would meet what he had come in search of: the recreation of a variant landscape, of a descending mask: snow. In a minute or two the sky would unclench and the first flakes fall like dull spangles, melting on his face, and lying on the frozen turf. It would be cheating if it did not snow. The wireless had reported that snow was lying on the Welsh hills, and the wind blew from that quarter. In half an hour's time he would be able to go back saying, 'It's snowing!'—a dramatic announcement; and imagining himself making it, he foresaw Helen's reaction: a glance at her brother and the exclamation, 'Poor creatures!' For the same news bulletin that reported the snow in Wales also reported the escape of two convicts from the prison that stood in the centre of the moor.

Such escapes were not uncommon; Uncle Bill declared that the prison authorities relied on them, as a chemical without which the men would rot into madness and despair. Those who made them only escaped from one captivity to another. The moor, shelterless, pathless, spread with quagmires, was a prison, and the farmers on its outskirts were jailers, since the men serving sentences had committed crimes of violence, and fear shut men's hearts against them. One reason why Uncle Bill was cold-shouldered by the farmers in the neighbourhood was that he had refused to join a party of convict-hunters who had come to his house in a cordial fox-hunting frame of mind, sure that he would join them. He and Helen were on the prisoners' side, as though it were an aspect of nature-loving, like being on the fox's side. That same morning Gilbert had watched Helen brushing and shaking a suit which had belonged to his father; and this, with a bottle of beer and a parcel of sandwiches, would be placed on the kitchen table that night, and the lamp left burning and the back door left open.

But no one would come. Even if the thousandth chance happened, and a prisoner on the run came down past the farm that stood alone in a cleft of the moor, and were to pause by the open door and see the clothes and the sand-wiches displayed, he would know better than to fall into so obvious a trap. Gilbert stubbed out his cigarette and prepared himself to go home reporting that he had seen a pair of buzzards. The snow would not come, either. With a noise like an explosion, a buzzard whirred up just behind him. He looked to see what had startled it, and saw a figure on the skyline. Silhouetted against the sky, it was huge and portentous. It descended into the dark surface of the moor, became invisible, reappeared as a dun-coloured upright insect, was swallowed up in a hollow, reappeared as a man who had no skill at such rough walking. 'My mother's convict,' thought Gilbert, and flattened himself into the contour of the rock. His mother's convict was making for the gate into the upper meadow. He was a smallish man, wearing a dirty raincoat that was too long for him.

Down in the farmhouse Helen must have been making up the fire, for a strong smell of wood-smoke puffed into the cold air. The man paused, snuffed it, and went on, hastening his steps. His gait had a shambling alertness, now that he walked on meadow grass.

The unbelievable was taking place under Gilbert's eyes, and he was the first to know of it. He raised himself cautiously, and saw the man pass into the lower meadow. The track would lead him directly into the yard, where Uncle Bill would be shutting up the ducks. Unless something went wrong at the last moment . . . As though in confirmation of his hopes, a cold feather of snow fell on his hand. He sat for ten minutes or so, mastering his ecstasy, and then walked home.

Helen was on the porch, and it was plain that she was waiting there to intercept him. 'I say! It's begun to snow,' he said. It was this he had planned to say. 'No? Has it?' Her voice exaggerated an interest she did not feel. She put her hand on his shoulder and bent down to whisper.

'Gilbert! We've got a visitor. Don't ask questions just now—but it's someone we have rather been expecting since this morning. He's having tea, and after that I expect he'll go to bed, for he's very tired, poor fellow! Don't stare at him, darling. And don't ask him anything. Just behave as if he were someone quite ordinary.'

She pushed him into the house and locked the door behind her. In the living-room the curtains were exactly drawn and Helen's geraniums were crowded into a hedge along the window-sill. The man, still wearing his raincoat, sat near the fire, holding a mug of tea which he shifted from hand to hand, warming the unoccupied hand before the blaze.

'It's only Gilbert, my son Gilbert,' Helen said.

The man half rose and said in a hasty mumbling voice, 'Pleased to meet you.'

'Pleased to meet you,' answered Gilbert, with a slight emphasis on the last word.

'We're all pleased,' said Helen quickly. 'Bill! That toast's burning.'

Uncle Bill turned the slice on the toasting-fork. His face had the same tautened expression as Helen's, but his movements were more composed; he did not appear, as she did, to be hatching a war-dance. When the toast was buttered, Helen said, 'Are you quite sure you wouldn't like a boiled egg?'

'Well, lady, since you've mentioned it again——'

'I should like an egg, too,' said Gilbert. Something unknown, ravishing, and disagreeable, had quickened in him. For the first time in his life he felt the jealousy of a son.

During tea most of the talking was done by Uncle Bill, who in a slow boring voice and with many reiterations told the stranger how isolated the farm was, and how they had learned to live without dependence on the outer world. As the kitchen clock began to strike, Gilbert switched on the wireless for the news bulletin. His mother had her convict, but he had his own private interest, and wanted to hear about the snow. She jumped up, and switched it off again.

'We won't have it to-night, Gilbert. I've got a head-ache.'

The stranger said sympathetically, 'I suffer with my head, too. Ever since I broke my nose in an accident, I've been liable to headaches. Never had them before.'

Looking at him across the table, Gilbert saw that his nose was markedly crooked. A nose like that would be a serious handicap to an escaping convict.

Early in the evening, the newcomer was hurried into the spare bedroom, where he would find a pair of pyjamas, Helen said, and other things he might need. They heard him moving about, and when his boots were off he padded like a bear. They heard the bed creak as he got into it, and presently they heard him snoring.

'The usual low mentality,' said Uncle Bill under cover of the snores. During the evening he and Helen had lost the air of moral elation they had worn earlier, and looked almost as though they were being hunted down themselves. With a sense of being kind and tactful, Gilbert began to read, and went to bed at the first suggestion he should do so. When he looked out of his window the snow was still falling.

By the morning, the snow was several inches deep and the rabbit hutches in the lower meadow looked like igloos. He was still hanging out of the window, entranced by the world new-modelled, when his mother came in, looking as if she had been up for hours.

'Darling.' she said—but her caress on his hair was inattentive—'Darling, there are one or two things I want to say to you before you come down to breakfast. They're rather important.'

'About the man?'

'Yes. About the man. First of all, while he's here, you mustn't turn on the wireless.'

'But don't you think he might want to know what's happening, and if the other man had been caught? I should. I should want to frightfully.'

'No, it wouldn't do at all. It would look as if we were trying to catch him out—watching him, you know. You see, Bill and I have been most careful to say nothing at all to him about—well, about what we assume. For us, he is just a stranger who had lost his way on the moor, and is very tired, and needs rest and kindness.'

'But suppose he asks me to turn it on?'

'You'd better say it's out of order. Yes, that's it. And I shall take out the battery. He knows already that we don't get a daily paper, so that's all right. The next thing is, don't go into his room. And don't say anything about his new clothes.'

'Won't my father's suit be much too large for him? —he's quite a small man. And frightfully old-fashioned?'

'We can't help that. Another thing, we must all think before we speak. I very nearly made the most awful blunder when he arrived, for I began to say, Won't you take off your coat? Uncle Bill only just saved me by saying it would dry best if he kept it on. And remember, Gilbert, he's going through a terrible strain. Don't make any sudden noises, don't do anything to startle him. We must all go on being as natural as possible.'

'Conceded. I'll talk about the snow, and the buzzards.'

'I'm not sure about buzzards. He would have seen them when he was *there*.'

'Well, the rabbits.'

At the door, she turned back and said, 'It's a privilege, a privilege, to be able to help a fellow-creature in such need! We ought to be thankful that he came to us.'

He had expected her to be more than thankful; he had expected her to be overjoyed, since it was what she had always wanted to happen. But grown-ups never enjoy things as much as they might.

'What's his name?'

'His name? Gilbert! We cannot possibly ask him his name.'

'Well, but we must call him something. You're always telling me not to call people You, because it's rude.'

'Good morning! Good morning! Hope you slept well.'

Uncle Bill's voice rang out loud and cheerful. The stranger's reply was inaudible. Then Uncle Bill began commenting on the snow, which would keep everyone housebound.

The snow continued to be a topic during breakfast. They all tried to be natural, and on the whole the stranger succeeded best, talking rather sentimentally about poor little wild birds and how they must be suffering. The suit was grotesquely too large for him, and grotesquely out of date, but he wore it with satisfaction, carefully removing every crumb that he dropped on it. He talked like a book, Gilbert noticed—like an old-fashioned book. Having evaded the works of Dickens, Rider Haggard, and Marryat, Gilbert saw no reason to endure them hashed up by a convict. He asserted as soon as possible his right to be useful out of doors. Instantly the stranger began to hoist himself from his chair.

'Bunnies, eh? Suppose I lend a hand? I bred rabbits at one time. They're second nature to me; I had over a hundred lop-ears and pouters, and one of my bucks got a highly commended at the Crystal Palace.'

'Don't go out!' Helen exclaimed, and amended it quickly, with, 'I wouldn't if I were you. You'll only spoil your suit.'

He sat down, looking crestfallen, but a minute later he was up again.

'Well then, I'll tell you what I'll do. I'll polish up all your brass for you, same as I did when I was in the Navy.'

When Gilbert came in to mid-day dinner the brass was not notably shinier, and his mother was calling the stranger Ernie.

After dinner, Ernie fell asleep and Helen sat down to spin. The sound of the wheel was like a small rivulet running through the house, a sound to carry away all care of mind. The snow cast an alien lighting into the room and made it look theatrical; everything was so like a stage-set, and she too, with her spinning wheel, that she felt a strong compulsion to sing. But what can one sing as one sits in a firelit snowbound room alone with a man who wishes to be called Ernie, a man of mean appearance and chirping childish egotism, who has raped, or robbed with violence, or slaughtered, and groped to the particular offence down a long tunnel of darkness and badness? And what was to be done with him? Snow had blinded the eyes of justice and filled up her scales with an impartial weight. But the snow would melt, and what was to be done then? If warders or searchers came to the door, it would be easy to know what to do: she would lie; if need be, she would shoot; she would pull a fringe of crime over herself, and no longer sit, manacled with guiltlessness, beside a man she could neither harm nor help. But suppose that no one came? What then? Her foot paused on the treadle, the wheel halted. As she stared at him, he opened his eyes.

'I am so thankful you are not out in this weather,' she said, speaking the truth of the minute.

'So am I, lady. I'd be a stiff by now, wouldn't I?'

He looked at her wheel.

'Spinning-wheel, isn't it? My old mother, she used to spin by the hour. She spun all my socks.'

'Really.'

It was all she could manage. During the morning she had heard a great deal about Ernie's mother, who baked her own bread, and kept geese and turkeys, and burned yule logs, and had been a lady's maid in such a grand house in Park Lane that in the lounge there was a golden fountain that sprayed out perfume when royalty dropped in for tea; who had geraniums and mongolias clambering all over the house, and worked her fingers to the bone for her family, and made Devonshire cream, and could tell fortunes by the cards, and cherished just such a vase, only it was a pair of them, as the Bernard Leach pitcher that Helen's husband had given her on their honeymoon. The mother recurred whenever Ernie lost interest in his demonstrations of being a Jack of all Trades, a handy Old Salt, a regular home-bird—demonstrations in which breakfast china was wiped with a paraffin rag, the brass candlesticks laved with metal-polish, breathed on, and replaced, rinsed kitchen towels wrung out with a gorilla's force by hands which had done a good job of black-leading, geraniums

watered till they overflowed, and potatoes left to steep in
bloodied water—for Ernie gashed his thumb while peeling
them, and peeled on, explaining that he had been about
too much to mind the sight of human blood. When it was
not his old mother, it was Susan, the spaniel bitch. Ernie
and Susan were bound to be pals, for Ernie could always
win a dog's heart and keep its respect too, a dog that didn't
respect a human being was a dog with no object in life,
and he didn't do it by tidbits either, he did it with the Eye,
something he'd got though he couldn't explain it. Susan,
with her high-bred spaniel's *nostalgie de la boue*, put no
strain on this occult gift. She licked, lolled, wagged, and
quivered, while Helen duly admired these devotional
exercises, and reminded herself that dogs discern goodness
of heart. During the morning she had managed not to feel
exasperated, being aided by the semi-unconsciousness of
having a hard morning's work to get through; but now,
because she was tired, because she had time to think,
because for a moment she had felt unforcedly the compassion she consciously maintained, Ernie's sock-spinning
old mother impinged on her as a nauseating sham. And
so she had frowned, and spoken coldly, and he, poor wretch,
had cowered. Ashamed, she set her wheel running again,
its voice so much kinder than hers. How could she be so
small-minded, so arbitrary in her judgements? Why should
a criminal be a good polisher, tidy, and the soul of truth?
How could she be so lacking in understanding?

Another question burst up through her self-reproaches.
Where had he stowed his convict's clothes? When she
went in to make his bed, though she had glanced about,
she had not seen them. Frightful garments, she did not
want to see them; but the question was still obsessing her

when Gilbert came in, ruddy with cold air and exercise. He had walked down to the village, and bought cigarettes and boiled sweets to give to Ernie. Helen now had more to reproach herself with. Failing so shockingly to understand Ernie, she had not understood her own child, either. She had thought that Gilbert was antagonistic to the stranger, resented his presence in the house, felt a plain scorn of him and a subtle scorn of her. She had been quite wrong. The sweets and the cigarettes were no flash-in-the-pan kindness, either. As the evening wore on it became obvious that the saturnine, private-minded Gilbert was laying himself out to be pleasant to Ernie, even to assuming a boyishness and warmth of manner which he ordinarily abjured; and if in the process he seemed rather condescending, that was because he was at the age when social graces are like new clothes, and don't have much give in them.

'What a rotten shame that the wireless should have gone bust just now, when we're snowed up, and you're here, and we'd like to put our best foot foremost. But I don't suppose there'd be any football results in this weather. Is there any team you specially follow?'

'Ah, now you've asked me something. But I don't mind admitting that I keep my eye on the Wolves.'

'Do you, do you? A very sound fancy, I'm sure. What do you think of——'

'When I can, that is,' interrupted Ernie. 'But I'm not always in circumstances so as I can give my whole attention to them, all through the season. As to-night, for instance. No radio.'

It seemed to Helen that Gilbert had flicked her with a glance of complicity; but he continued smoothly, blamelessly. 'And what other things do you like listening to? The Archers? Dance music? Classical music?'

Now Gilbert was really going too far. But on the contrary; Ernie looked intensely gratified, and when he replied there was a new purposefulness in his boasting.

'Well, it may surprise you, but I'm all for what's classical. Specially hymns. There's nothing to beat a real good old hymn. There's a drawing power about a hymn. . . . Stands to reason, don't it? It's what they're meant for. It's like I always say—a bloke what can stand up and sing a hymn, and put in the shades of expression, you understand, that bloke's got something in the kitty what the world can't take away.'

Gilbert said fervently, 'I'm sure you can sing.'

'There's many as has said so in the past. And when I was a boy, no bigger than you, I sung solos in a surplice at Westminster Abbey. And the Brompton Ororatory. But my voice isn't what it was, it's been through too much. A constancy of wet feet, not to dwell on all I've been through and the teeth I've lost, will knock the mellowness out of any voice.'

'I expect you can put more shades of expression in, though, with all you've been through. Do let's do a hymn! You sing, and I'll vamp.'

'I don't know that I can do myself justice.'

Gilbert opened the cottage piano, and strummed a few impassioned chords. 'Come on, now! What shall it be?'

Ernie rose to his feet, raised his eyebrows, drew a long wheezy breath, and then burst with a tremolo yell like a beginning bagpipe's into *Lead Kindly Light*.

Helen had never been able to understand why the

music-master at Gilbert's school should have written such very enthusiastic reports about Gilbert's remarkable talent. At home, Gilbert's talent manifested itself by the extreme captiousness with which he listened to broadcasts by really good pianists, a flat refusal to practise scales or play pieces, and complaints that the piano was out of tune again. Now, half willingly, half grudgingly, she acknowledged the *savoir-faire* and agility with which Gilbert tracked down Ernie's uncertain wanderings from key to key, adapted himself to Ernie's habit of dwelling on any note where he could do himself justice, and reinforced the shades of expression by putting in corroborative effects with flawless vulgarity and dexterity, deepening the darkness with a chromatic bass, making the day more garish with glissandos, and closing with such a coruscation of angel faces smiling that her baser emotions almost swept her into thinking, 'But this is beautiful', when with all her principles she knew it was abominable. It was a relief to her feelings when Ernie caught his accompanist napping by singing a loud sudden Amen just as Gilbert's hands had finally fluttered themselves off the keyboard to dangle at his sides in executive exhaustion.

'Bravo, bravo! *Bis, bis!*' exclaimed the accompanist. 'What shall we do next? *Onward, Christian Soldiers? Star of the Sea?*'

Ernie chose *Star of the Sea*. Gilbert's left hand surged and billowed, and his right hand threw in some touching allusions to church counterpoint. It was, as Ernie allowed after his solo Amen (apparently Gilbert had been taken by this effect), very nice.

'Oh, thank you!'

'Thank *you*.'

'Not at all. I adore vamping. And *Star of the Sea* is such a catching tune, don't you think?'

'It's a good hymn. But it doesn't suit me, not like the other does. And what shows it, is the dog. She never made to howl more than once or twice. It didn't touch her in the same way.'

The indication was plain. *Lead, Kindly Light* was repeated, and again repeated.

When the performers had gone to bed, Bill said, 'Well, there's one grain of truth in the poor chap's mountebanking. I should say he undoubtedly did sing solos in a surplice. Most likely that's what set him off. Choir-boys notoriously go to the bad.'

'What makes you think he was ever able to sing? He's got no voice, he's got no ear.'

'He's got what Gilbert has, he's got performance. He expects to be listened to.'

'If it hadn't been so agonizing, and so agonizingly funny, it would have been pathetic.'

'And you would have dropped a shilling into the hat. He's been a choir-boy, Helen. And he's sung in the street. How the poor devil stinks!'

Bill opened the window. The light shone on a flurry of snowflakes, falling in a wandering, dancing descent. Even as she watched, the flakes grew larger and fell more purposefully. In the room that had been so full of sham and shindy they now heard only the solemn boom of the north wind. 'This will go on all night,' said Bill. 'Well, all the better for our purpose.'

'Bill! What *is* our purpose? What are we to do about this man?'

'Feed him, keep him indoors, keep him warm, build

him up for when he's on the run again. We can't do more.'

'It seems so little, so very little for anything that is so taxing. And he's such a poor braggart, and so silly!—as silly as a fly in the milk, and he makes me feel just as impatient and just as responsible. When you opened the window, I thought of all our creatures, old Diamond in the stable, and the cows, and the hens sleeping on their perch in a row, and the rabbits—all so safe and so ordinary. One feels such guilt, Bill!'

'Worrying ahead won't make it any better, my dear. Take a leaf out of Ernie's hymnbook: "I do not ask to see the distant scene; one step enough for me." We'd better take these geraniums off the window-sill or they'll be frosted by the morning.'

Bill had been educated at a public school, and hymns were part of his heritage, he would sing them while currying Diamond or gelding little pigs. Helen had not been thus immunized. As rendered by Ernie and Gilbert, *Lead, Kindly Light* had seemed only a springboard for their joint exhibitionism; but Bill's quotation had authenticated it, and as she lay in bed, trying not to worry, trying to get to sleep, it began to trickle into her consciousness like an oil— smooth, pervasive, inescapable; an oil that had purged itself from the scum of those repeated performances, each more sentimental and meretricious than the last.

> *Lead, kindly light, amid the encircling gloom,*
> *Lead thou me on.*
> *The night is dark and I am far from home . . .*

She discovered that she was word-perfect in it. Ernie could not sing, but his diction was commanding; he got his words over as plain as print, and uttered them as though they were his own, as though they had never been pronounced except in his flat wet voice and cockney accent. It was Ernie who amid encircling gloom stumbled towards a light, and with all the force of his self-importance felt assured of its kindliness, its good intentions towards him.

> *So long thy power hath blest me, sure it still*
> *Will lead me on . . .*

Where to? Where to, after he had been built up to go on the run again? Where to, and for what end, poor Ernie, with his shambling gait and his strutting imagination, zigzagging from chance to chance, keeping his heart up with boasts, bedizening his destitution with old mothers and pouter rabbits which had been highly commended at the Crystal Palace. He was not likely to get very far; a broken nose and a suit so much too large for him would denounce him to watchers and tale-bearers almost as plainly as the broad arrows would. He should never have been given that suit, and somehow it must be replaced by something less conspicuous. In the reports of captures, the escaped prisoners usually said they were glad to be picked up, salvaged from hunger and exposure and insecurity, and these reports might be convincing, if one did not remember that the same men had desperately escaped. She fell into an uneasy sleep, and dreamed that she was searching for Ernie's convict clothes; but while she was searching, the dream slipped into a deeper preoccupation, and it was Ernie's crime she was searching for, which was somehow bundled up in the clothes; finding the one, she would find the other. She sought in darkness, but that did not impede the search, since clothes and crime would give out a phosphorescent light, like bad fish.

She wrenched herself awake. The night was dark and he was far from home. Those were his snores that she heard. A man who snored like that would never be able to sleep unmolested in a barn—unless he were taken for a screech-owl, or a ghost. These desolate strangling outcries came from the midnight's Ernie, the Ernie who could no longer shelter himself in brag and tinsel imaginations of all the fine things he had done and been; for in the darkness his crime came up and seized him like a gaoler whose hold could not be bought off by the serving of any sentence. 'This sham of justice!' she exclaimed aloud. Silence retorted, 'This sham of mercy.' When Bill uttered those words, 'when he is on the run again', she had felt an unmasterable sense of relief. It had gone, and now she felt only woe; but the sense of relief had only gone into hiding, and would recur. So there was nothing to be done but to follow Bill's advice, and concentrate on making Ernie warm, well-fed, and happy. In pursuing this, the rest of the household would be warm and well-fed and happy too; it was all she was fit to aim at.

*

By the light of bleak dawn, this appeared a more considerable undertaking. But after the first hour, during which she had the house pretty much to herself and only routine obligations to comply with, her spirits rose into that kind of weakly elation that people feel when they have put a sleepless night behind them. It seemed to her that the breakfast table with its clean cloth and blue china looked delightfully spruce, that the loaf she sliced had a particularly fine close texture, that bacon and coffee had never smelt more beguiling on a cold morning. It was all she could do not to draw attention to this breakfast casketed like a jewel in the warm room, with snow and grey skies everywhere around. Such fancies were soon quenched. Bill was preoccupied. The snow had drifted in the lane so that he could not get the milk churns down to the stand, and Treacle, their best Jersey cow, was mysteriously ailing. Ernie had dreamed of cockroaches, a sure omen of bad luck. Gilbert came down when everything had got cold, and ate with an air of grievance.

'What about some music?' she said when she had at last dislodged him from brooding over coffee grounds. 'You won't disturb me in the least, and I shall be out of your way. As Ernie is here I am going to make a chocolate cake, the special one with raisins. You like it, don't you, Gilbert?'

'Not now.'

Black looks followed her when she went out with the tray. Gilbert was fomenting his jealousy; it was less ravishing now that it was no longer a new sensation, but obsessively entertaining, like a game of skill at which he was growing better and better. Ernie was slighted at the suggestion that he should sing without an audience. When she went in to make up the fire, they were playing Beggar my Neighbour. There were several things that Gilbert might have been doing, but she said nothing of them, since he was so well employed in keeping Ernie happy. But apparently Ernie was not being kept happy. At her reappearance he jumped up and became that Jack of all Trades who had dogged her through the previous morning. By the time the mid-day dinner was on the table, Helen was reeling with exhaustion, headache, and the effort of not snapping. The sky had cleared, the room was full of the harsh whiteness of sunlight reflected off snow; it stabbed her short-sighted eyes and denounced every smear, every trail of cigarette ash, every item of the disorder and sluttishness that proliferated from Ernie's presence in the house. 'You look fagged,' commented Bill. 'You'd better have a nap this afternoon. Ernie will help you wash up.' Delivered over to the tormentor, she agreed with a grateful smile.

She felt too tired for anything so positive as repose, and pulled out her spinning-wheel. The small rivulet began to flow, but this time it was not she who felt an impulse to sing. Ernie had secured an audience.

'Feeling a bit low, aren't you? No wonder, cooped up in this dead-alive spot. So suppose we give you a little concert, to pass the time and brighten things up?'

She looked imploringly at Gilbert. There was no mercy in his answering grimace of condolence. Suddenly she saw a possible expedient.

'Gilbert, have you finished painting those shelves in the loft yet?' She knew that he hadn't, and did not wait to be answered. 'Well, I think you must do it this afternoon.'

'There's no hurry. I've got plenty of time before I go back.'

'But I haven't. I want to put the jam pots away. Off with you, Gilbert. I'm serious.'

For if I knock his accompanist from under him, she thought, Ernie won't sing. It proved even better, for Ernie, saying that if he could be given a rag and a comb he would show Gilbert how to marble, he had taught marbling to a man who had marbled a whole suite for the Archbishop of Canterbury, went off to the loft too. She went on spinning, hollowing her mind to become merely a vessel for the wheel's gentle murmur to fill and overbrim. The wheel grew heavier as the skein gathered on it, the murmur deepened, and when she broke off to piece her yarn the noise seemed to flow on and on. Twice she pulled herself back from falling asleep. When next she opened her eyes, the room seemed to be swimming with blood—blood on the walls, and dyeing the wool on her spindle. As she saw it, the blood faded, fading with the reflection of the sunset that was dying out in the western sky. She must have been asleep for nearly two hours. Her limbs were cramped, her mind was cramped too; she could not unstiffen it from the shock of waking in a room full of blood. She put on the kettle, a composing act. The icy air that came in through the ill-fitting kitchen window made her think penitently of Gilbert and Ernie in the loft.

The loft was over the woodshed, and approached by an exterior flight of stone steps. She went to the foot of the steps and called. There was no answer. She went up the steps and looked in. The loft was empty. 'They're some-where with Bill,' she said to herself. Poor Bill! She searched about for him; he was nowhere in the farm buildings. She listened, but there was no sound of voices. He's going round the rabbits, she thought, and turned towards the gate into the lower meadow. A man, quite motionless, was looking over the wall. The wall hid him, all but his head and shoulders. He was wearing a felt hat, round his neck was a muffler, and like Maigret, he had a pipe in his mouth—she could see the angular black pattern against the white blur of his face. It was a plain-clothes detective, keeping watch.

Helen was naturally timid, and in any emergency her

impulse was to rush headlong towards the danger, since her instinct was to run away. She ran up the yard, slipping and skidding on the trampled snow. The man did not stir. He was a snow man.

A moment later, two other heads rose above the level of the wall, and were Ernie and Gilbert. 'Quite a surprise, eh?' said the one. 'We thought some outdoor exercise would be good for us,' said the other. 'When we saw you come out, we ducked, and waited.'

'You didn't do much painting,' she said. Her voice was so metallically composed that they were quelled, and followed her sheepishly back to the house. I have gone through all this for nothing, she thought; for in the moment between staring into the snow man's white idiot face and confronting the idiot flushed faces that rose on either side of it, she had seen two men riding up the moor. They were the two Smurdens, sons of a local farmer, carrying fodder to their moor ponies, and from their mounts they would have had a good instructive view of Ernie.

She had gone through all this for nothing; and moreover, the Smurdens' instructive view of Ernie was her fault. This second consideration had worked its way uppermost by the time Bill came in. He had ridden down to the village to consult the vet about Treacle by telephone. Sellenger had been reassuring, he said. Bill's treatment was correct, Treacle should soon recover, there was nothing to worry about.

'Quite a weight off your mind,' commented Ernie, and added perfunctorily, 'Poor thing!'

'Yes, indeed.'

'Though I suppose if it isn't one thing, it's another, and if there's nothing else, then it's the weather. Never a farmer without a grumble, so they say. It's proverbial, isn't it? Well, it's a world of troubles. Not that I'm that way myself, I believe in being cheerful. I'm renowned for it. I knew a farmer once, he was in a big way, a dairy farmer in Surrey, and made those whopping great Stilton cheeses; he sent a cheese every Christmas to the President of America and did everything by electricity—well, believe it or not, he asked me to go down there whenever I could spare the time—I was acting in the films then, character parts—just to walk round at milking time being cheerful. He said it put half as much cream again on the milk. Psychological, you know.'

Ernie had glided away into his world of boast and romance; but when he spoke of 'one thing and another' it was as though he shared with Helen an impression that Bill's relief about Treacle was counterpoised by some other reason to be worried. Bill must have seen the snow man, and the Smurdens riding by on the moor. When he went out for another look at Treacle, she followed him.

'It was my fault. I was frantic to get rid of them, so I let them go to the loft. I should never have put so much responsibility on Gilbert.'

'Well, what happened?'

'Didn't you see the snow man? They went out and made a snow man just outside the meadow gate. And they must have been seen, for the two Smurdens were carrying up hay for the ponies.'

'H'm! That's a pity. Gilbert's got a bad attack of swelled head.'

'He's too young to remember our responsibility. I should have remembered for him.'

'His head is swelled. Thank heaven, he'll soon be gone! —Gilbert, I mean. Treacle is certainly on the mend— aren't you, my girl? Sellenger laughed at me for thinking it might be foot and mouth.'

'Did you think that? Bill, how frightful!'

'One always has it at the back of one's mind.'

The reprieve, even from an imagined danger, of these innocent creatures affected her with an absolving straight-forward quality of poetry, so that to go back from the cow-shed to the house seemed like quitting a temple for a Bedlam. But the remainder of the evening was not so bad as she feared. After a brace of hymns Bill announced that he would read aloud, and opened William Morris's *Earthly Paradise* at the story of Ogier the Dane. Gilbert and Ernie fidgeted, offering each other cigarettes, tossing each other the matchbox, officiously leaping up and down to feed the fire, but he read on inflexibly. She thanked him as she said goodnight, adding that she would try to be more rational to-morrow. 'Don't worry about to-morrow,' he said, in a withdrawn voice which must mean he was worried him-self. Standing in her bedroom, too tired to undress, she found herself wishing that Bill and she were man and wife; for then they would lie darkened in the one bed, telling each other what troubled them, and expressing things one can never express when in one's clothes and by day. She would talk about Ernie, and about Gilbert, over whom her conscience was becoming almost as disagreeable as Gilbert himself had become. He would talk about Treacle. Neither would do much to comfort the other, and yet both would be comforted. She saw from the window that the snow was lying as though it had always lain and would lie for ever. The snow man looked over the wall with his humped shoulders and the pipe frozen in his white pudding-face.

On the other side of the house Ernie was also taking a look at the snow; but as his disposition was more sanguine than Helen's he was thinking that it couldn't last much longer, and that in a couple of days he would get away. Not that he disliked his lodging: the tea was hot and strong, the eggs were really fresh; though the mattress was hardish there were plenty of blankets; though the gent and lady were a bit dim you could see at a glance that they wouldn't harm a fly; young Gilbert had cottoned to him, and the dog was a real pal. Also, it was a good suit of clothes. So he had nothing against his lodging, and it had come in very handy, just when he could do with a few days in a peaceful spot. Lucky again! Lucky Ernie! It's better to be lucky than clever. But now he wanted to be moving along, for there comes a time when the best of friends must part. We pass by this way but once, as Jesus Christ said, so while you're at it, do all the good turns you can. Ever a guiding motto, and no one could say he hadn't lived up to it while here, what with the brass polished, and the grate black-leaded, and the geraniums watered daily, poor things, they didn't half need it for they were just about dying for lack of a drink—which he had remarked on, but no one had taken up the hint, nothing, after the first bottle of swipes, but tea and thimblefuls of that hairwash the lady called home-made wine—and the fire kept an eye on, and the scullery work done without a murmur, and the boy brought out of himself and made playful, and the best part of every helping of cake given to the dog; not to mention keeping the con-versation going to liven things up, and singing hymns which no one could object to. So he would have nothing to reproach himself with when he moved along—which might be almost any time now, he decided, once more snuffing the air with an experienced nose before shutting the window and wadding with a sock the place where the air got in. 'That's all right. Gor bless,' he mumbled, falling blamelessly asleep. It did not occur to him to take into his calculations the fact that he had been received with a rather unusual degree of kindness. Having little experience of kindness, he did not think it an unusual degree. It was the sort of thing he often fancied coming his way, when he was not fancying himself bestowing kindness on a much grander scale.

*

In the middle of the night Helen woke up with a start of fear. Listening for footsteps, groans, cries for help, and hearing nothing but the wind, she realized it was the wind that frightened her. It had gone round to the south-west. There would be a thaw.

The first daylight showed her a darkening landscape. Where the snow still lay it had lost its ample contours, and looked cadaverous. The gutters were overflowing, the pipe had fallen from the snow man's mouth. She tried not to think about leaks in the roof, but while she was brushing her hair a drip fell between her and the looking-glass. The before-breakfast chores were ten times heavier and more protracted. She slopped and waded through them in a dull frenzy, thinking all the time of the Smurdens riding up the moor. Soon now men looking for Ernie would come to the house. Because they had relied on that treacherous snow, no plans had been made, nothing was agreed upon. It must be tackled immediately after breakfast. Nothing could be

tackled before breakfast, because Susan had run away, and
Ernie pursued her saying that, whatever it cost him, he
would find her; he had a way of whistling that would
recall any lady-dog.

Helen was hacking at kindling in the woodshed, inter-
minably waiting to catch Bill for a word of sense, when he
and Ernie walked past. She heard him say that he would
like to learn that whistle, and that they could look round
for Susan at the same time. She realized with a stagger of
relief that Bill was tackling it. Ernie was being taken to a
hiding-place. He was wearing his raincoat and Bill was
carrying a rush bag that bulged. Now for the clothes! They
must be got rid of, destroyed! She ran indoors, swept past
Gilbert, and dashed upstairs. Ernie's room smelled like
some imprisoned animal's den—an animal whose diet was
cigarettes, whose bedding was toffee-wrappers. The bedclothes sprawled on the floor. A pillow had been dis-
mantled and its pillow-case, folded and refolded into a
grimy oblong no larger than an envelope, lay amid crumbs
on the mattress. A hunted animal so recently an imprisoned
animal—no wonder his room smelt like a den! She opened
the window—the catch was so sticky that she dabbled her
hand in the drips from the gutter to cleanse it—and began
her search. Not in the closet. Not in the three upper
drawers of the bureau. She pulled at the bottom drawer,
remembering quite well that it was locked, because she kept
her summer dresses in it and in her hasty arraying of the
room for Ernie she had locked the drawer because they
looked so tauntingly carefree. It opened, letting out the
mother-essence of the stink that filled the room. Ernie's
clothes, rolled up sodden and filthy, had been shoved in on
top of her summer dresses. He must have thrust them in

just as they came off him, only taking time to pick the lock. Presumably he meant to lock the drawer again, and so conceal them; such a thought was on a par with his hapless stupidity. Well, she must do better than that! As she hauled them out she saw that the trousers were greasy grey flannel, the coat a cheap tweed. They were civilian clothes.

A voice from the doorway said, 'Perhaps he got them off a scarecrow.'

'Gilbert, how silly! You could search the whole moor and not find a scarecrow. Who wants to scare crows off stone and heather? Do try to sharpen your wits. We may need them.'

'Poor Gilbert, the fool of the family . . . always jumping to conclusions.'

When Gilbert wished to charm, he referred to himself in the third person. She paid no heed to the wish.

'I can't make it out. But wherever he got them, I must burn them.'

'Yes. It would be a prudent step, a hygienic step. He won't need them. He has risen above them. He has gone on his way to the village in my father's suit.'

'To the village?'

'Look,' said Gilbert, fluting the word.

Looking from the window she saw Ernie tripping jauntily down the track, swinging the rush bag, and hopping over the puddles. And Bill was walking towards the house. Now he'll go and look at Treacle, she thought; and felt such an onslaught of despair and fatigue that she sat down on the bed. Gilbert hallooed from the window, adding, 'Helen's found Ernie's clothes, and she's about to pass out.'

She heard Bill run upstairs. He came into the room with a look on his face that was partly merry and partly embarrassed. 'Well, Helen, I see you've guessed it. Ernie has gone off without a stain on his character. He was a tramp, an old-fashioned, bred-in-the-bone tramp. I gave him some money, and some socks, and cut him some sandwiches, and showed him how to get on to the main road, and now he's gone. He was rather glad to go.'

'How did you guess?'

'I never got quite so far as a guess, though I was beginning to think we were mistaken. Then, yesterday evening, when I rode down to ring up Sellenger from the post-office, Mrs. Mudge—detestable woman!—began to prate about being able to sleep in peace again, and told me how she had spent all Tuesday praying that the two convicts might be caught, and that they'd been rounded up that same night, and didn't it show what prayer can do? Pah!'

'You knew this yesterday evening?'

'Yes, Helen, I did. But I wanted to get him out of the way before I told you. I thought it would save awkwardness. After all, it was in no way the poor fellow's fault. I invited him in, you remember, and it had begun to snow; and he took it pretty much for granted. Tramps are like nuns in that way; they have a very narrow acquaintance with real life.'

'I wonder how he came to be on the moor. Tramps stay on roads.'

'As it happens, he told me. He—he thought he saw those convicts, ran for his life, and lost himself.'

Gilbert exploded into laughter. He laughed with such savagery that she turned about, ready to wreak her nerves on him. 'Gilbert! Did you guess this?'

'Guess it? Good Lord, no! *I knew*. I knew it the day after he arrived. For that afternoon, while you and he were being Faust and Marguerite round the spinning wheel, I skipped down to the shop and bought some sweets and told them you had sent me to enquire as our wireless wasn't working. That's how I found out. It had been on the eight o'clock News. After all,' he continued, answering her silence, 'someone in the house has to know something.'

'And you didn't tell us?'

'I wasn't asked.'

'I call it vulgar, vulgar and contemptible!' she exclaimed. 'I feel put to shame by such behaviour. Yes, Gilbert, I do. Don't you know that that sort of thing is just sniggering, and that no self-respecting person sniggers, any more than they would laugh at a blind beggar.'

'Well, as it happens, I often laugh at blind beggars. I make a habit of it. I find it very amusing. Even when the blind beggar is my own mother, begging up to a half-witted tramp, just like Susan, I still find it amusing. And I'd like to know what else I could have done. I didn't want to break up your romance. You'd always wanted a convict, you thought you'd got one, you were all of a twitter about him; if I hadn't twittered too, you'd have felt put to shame by my behaviour. Anyhow, you didn't ask me. It didn't occur to you to ask me. You were too busy being a mother to Ernie, baking special cakes for him, warming his feet, sparing his feelings, listening to his lies and his clap-trap as if he was the Archangel Gabriel, lying awake all night to cry over him, thanking him for being so kind as to wear my father's clothes, listening to his revolting hymns, making his beastly bed. . . . Who was I to rout you out of your love's young dream? And if I had tried, I would have needed to take a sledge-hammer to make you notice me. I should have thought I made it sufficiently obvious that I knew he was an impostor, but all you saw was your simple kind-hearted little boy, fetching footstools for him, handing him more sugar, vamping accompaniments for him on the old Pi-ah-no. Yes, I saw you, giving me a kind grin from time to time, thinking that Gilbert was learning to be understanding at last. Understanding! I should think I was understanding. I was so understanding that I was ready to throw up. Not that I minded. On the contrary, I enjoyed every moment of it. I've never seen such fools all fooling each other all the time, I wouldn't have missed such an experience for the world. I've never enjoyed a holiday so much before.'

He raged, and she sat on the bed, relaxing, reviving, expanding like a flower. Her cheeks grew pink, her eyes brightened, her lips parted, her expression was at once timid and triumphant, the expression of a young girl who suddenly finds herself swimming, safe as a fish, in the billows of sexual wrath and sexual jealousy. He raged himself out, and stood trembling like a song-bird, trapped, and exposed, and aghast; and even then she mercilessly, silently, went on enjoying it. At last, in a voice sleek and meek as a virgin's, she said, 'Gilbert, you really are the most odious youth. I've never been so insulted in all my life.'

Fished out of his agony, he scrambled to the dry land of every day.

'It was pretty good, wasn't it? But you deserved every word of it. I don't know how a woman called Helen could sink so low.'

'Pull me up,' she said, holding out her hands. 'Goodness,

I'm tired! I feel as if I'd been dragged through a hedge backward. Well—it's all over.'

Bill, seeing what the upshot of their quarrel would be, had gone to look out of the window, making notes to himself of where the gutters were blocked. Now he turned back and said with great kindness, 'Yes, it's over. We've all made fools of ourselves, and now I think we ought to crack a bottle of Helen's wine.'

'And drink to Ernie,' added Gilbert. 'May his top notes never grow less! I hope you appreciated my angel faces smiling? Tweedle-weedle! Did you notice how I lost them awhile by modulating down a semitone? By the way, Ernie was so touched by my genius that he gave me his photograph as a souvenir.'

He had kept this blinding ace up his sleeve. Now he displayed it. It was a snapshot, enlarged to postcard size, of Ernie, standing at a pavement's edge and brandishing a tambourine. It was unmistakably Ernie, with his mean foolish face and his gap-toothed grin, but he was dressed as a woman, with a low-necked bodice and a blonde wig. Gilbert handed it to Helen, calmly, as though it were nothing to him, and waited for the result.

She glanced at it, and began to laugh. Her laughter was spontaneous and perfectly untrammelled.

'O Bill, look at this! You were quite right. He must have been a choirboy.'

It was not at all what Gilbert had expected.

For three intolerable days while the spectacle of Helen making a fool of herself was inciting him to feel hourly more sophisticated, more sardonic, more like an uncle, a less respectable frame of mind had swept him in the contrary direction, making him feel hourly more deprived, more suspicious, more frantic, more like a baby that yells itself black in the face. Nothing like this must ever happen again. The mother who could arouse such jealousy, the Helen newly discovered as being so much dearer than he supposed, was nevertheless still the same foolish creature, top-heavy with high ideals and unworldly as a rabbit. If nothing like this was to happen again, she must be got under control. His control—after all, he was her natural guardian, or soon would be. It was his duty, a duty he was ready and willing to take on himself, to watch over her, and protect her, and always be on very good terms with her while always retaining a dash of that sophisticated uncle. Now, in this moment of truth, was the time to establish this new relationship. And so he had produced that ghastly photograph, reckoning on it to do the trick. She had taken it, not only without flinching (he had flinched), but with laughter and unconcern.

She handed the photograph back to him, and he took it with a little bow. She was his superior, for she was adult. Acknowledging this with uncompetitive esteem, Gilbert resolved to become adult as soon as he possibly could.

DURING A WINTER NIGHT

———————

At any rate, they should find it all clean and tidy.

So a little after 11 p.m., at an hour when normally she would have emptied the sink basket, washed through the dishcloths, turned the kettle upside down, and gone to bed, Florence Cullen made herself a pot of strong tea preparatory to giving the kitchen a thorough turnout. For this once, she could take her time over it, and do it to her own satisfaction—the walls and ceiling broomed, the range blacked, the larder scrubbed, drawers and cupboards relined with clean paper, the gas cooker scoured with hot soda suds. No one would interrupt her, and as the kitchen was in the basement she would disturb no one. Overhead was the front parlour, now referred to as the lounge. Her daughter Jennifer, whose bedroom was behind it, had gone to a party, saying she did not expect to get back much before the milk. Sheila, her other daughter, with Tom and their four children lay sleeping on the first floor; her son Jasper, his Peggy, and the twins were above them; Mr. Laver, the lodger, was tossing and turning in the attic. She knew he was a poor sleeper, for her bedroom was next to his. Through the thin wall she often heard him walking up and down, banging the window open or shut, drumming his fingers on the tabletop, and sighing like a horse. She bore him no resentment. He was a man who intended no harm to anyone and he had been kind to her old cat, even buying shrimps for it, which, considering how stingy he was and how frightened of spending money, showed a good heart.

It would take all of three hours, she told herself as she sat deliberately finishing the last drop of tea. Well, that would be just about right. It would fill in the time nicely. Having consulted the tea leaves for omens—a gentleman visitor—she rolled up her sleeves, tied on her coarse apron, and began to clear the room. As she went to and fro she was dogged by a sense of oddity and solemnity; she seemed to be moving objects whose weight and function were unknown to her. But from the moment of raising her broom and dislodging the first cobweb from the ceiling, everything became as usual. She was Florence Cullen, giving her kitchen a thorough turnout, and not before it needed it, either. As she worked on, the noises of a thorough turnout, the clatter of the bucket, the harsh purr of the scrubbing brush, neighboured and encouraged her. It was as though they were making talk, with nothing new to say but keeping up conversation just to pass the time and ward off the growing silence after midnight.

But now their talk was at an end. The broom, having swept the floor, the scrubbing brush and the swab, having gone over every inch of it, the cheerful bucket—they had finished their work and been put away. Only the polishing remained. While she waited for the lino to dry, her thoughts stretched upward through the house of sleeping people who would all be there in the morning, and settled with a sensation almost of repose on Mr. Laver. It was to be hoped that Sheila would not raise the rent or turn him out, poor ageing young fellow!

With a start, she noticed that the lino was dry. It would take a good half-hour to polish it; then the furniture that she had moved into the passage must be moved back again; then there would be no more to do. When the lino was

new she could whisk over it in no time, but as lino wears
out it swallows more polish, and more rubbing is needed to
get a proper gloss. There was a lot of it, for it was a big
kitchen. Twenty-three years ago, when Jerome came in
saying he'd been looking over an empty house in Alma
Road and meant to offer for the lease, this big kitchen had
been one of his boasts. 'A real gentry kitchen, old girl.
Turtle soup, and haunches of venison, and all that. And
such a larder, with a marble slab, and hooks. Oh, you'll be
in your glory.' And she had laughed at him, asking, 'What's
wrong with Buckingham Palace?' But he was serious, he
had everything worked out. Alma Road, being, though still
respectable, a gone-down-in-the-world neighbourhood,
just suited his books, since it is in such a neighbourhood
that people need a builder and decorator who'll undertake
small repairs. The house had been standing empty, and was
in bad order, so he would get it reasonable, and since he
would be doing the repairs himself, they would cost nothing beyond the materials.

This was in February, and on Easter Sunday she was
hanging curtains, with a leg of lamb in the oven. It was a
semi-basement house, with a flight of steps leading to the
front door, and a tradesmen's entrance with another flight
of steps going down into the area. Jerome had his office and
showroom on the ground floor, so the family used the
tradesmen's entrance. It was a fine roomy area, with space
and light enough for potted plants, geraniums and ferns,
and a canary vine on strings. She and Jerome sat there on
summer evenings, he with his pipe, she with her sewing, or
a book of poetry. She had always been one for poetry. To
herself, she called the area 'my bower'.

In the second winter of the war, the bomb that hit the

public house at the street corner toppled the next-door chimney through their roof and blew out all the windows. In no time, Jerome had a tarpaulin on the roof, wire mesh in the windows, and a placard saying 'BUSINESS AS USUAL' over the broken fanlight of the office door. A week later, that notice had to come down. He was out on duty as an air-raid warden when a splinter of plate glass cut his throat. It had been a fearful night, listening to the bombs coming down and the shells going up. The three children were asleep in the shelter Jerome had made under the kitchen stairs, and she was boiling a kettle on the primus, since the gas was off again, when young Martindale came in to break the news. The kettle boiled while he was telling her what a loss Jerome would be at the A.R.P. post, and she had made tea, just as if nothing had happened, saying 'Since you're here, you'd better stay for a cup.' He had stayed, and before he left he had asked her to marry him.

Much later on, when the children were growing up and growing beyond her, she sometimes wondered how things would have turned out if she had consented. But at the time she knew the offer for what it was worth: a first-aid kindness, born of the desperate moment. When she met him a few days later, he looked at her with no more recollection of his words than if they had been spoken in a fever. Life was like that then; you were matter-of-fact when you were crazy, you were crazy when you were matter-of-fact, imperilling your life to keep your place in a queue for quarter of a pound of biscuits, sleeping in the bowels of the earth because it was healthier, and pouring scornful pity on the dull wretches who had left London for the safety of the country. Only the other day Beryl Cohen had said, as they

came away together from the bag-wash laundry, 'No one
seeing us now would think what a larky lot we were in the
war.'

'Easy to be larky when you've got nothing worse than
death on your tracks. It's the real life sentence, year in,
year out—that's what puts paid to larkiness.'

She was not aware how much rancour had spurted out
in her words till she saw Beryl Cohen draw away as if a
mad dog had snapped at her. But it was different for Beryl
Cohen. Her boy was a Jew and stood up for his mother.

Moving backwards as she polished, Florence now edged
herself on her knees through the passage. Scrub towards the
sink, polish towards the door—she had learned this rule
from her mother and abided by it ever since. Nowadays,
you had only to advise a daughter to do it one way and she'd
do it the diametrical opposite—or else not do it at all and
say it wasn't necessary. 'Mum, why on earth put bread
through the mincer to clean it? There's no need to, you've
got detergents.' 'Oh, Mum, not dusting the dresser again?'
'I don't see why you bother to make marmalade, except it
gives you an excuse to hoard up jam pots.' 'Mum wouldn't
think a pie legal unless she's made patterns round it with a
fork.' 'Oh, Mum, do for God's sake chuck this wash-up-
as-you-go business. Leave them in the sink and do the lot
in the morning.' 'If Mum could have her way, she'd put
the kids to bed at half past six and then sing lullabies to
them.'

She sat back on her heels, and surveyed the polished
floor. It looked lovely, it really did. So did the old range,
and the brass taps over the sink, and the wooden pot board
beneath the dresser, scrubbed with salt and whitening like
a beach. If she had had her own way, she would have gone

on using the range, with its two ovens and wide top where there was room for half a dozen saucepans—old-fashioned iron saucepans that would keep simmering on, and no trouble to anybody. During the early days she had always used it for Sunday dinners, thinking of the turtle soup and the haunches of venison and the gentry cook working her pastry on the marble slab. Such things are not poetical, yet she had felt a sort of poetry in her thoughts. The long frost of 1947 cracked the chimney, and no one would hear of repairing it—Sheila talking of the price of coal, and Jasper saying that she could not possibly clean the flues because of her bad heart; so now there was only the gas cooker, with Sheila and Peggy twitching each other's pots off the flame and quarrelling. But at this moment, how peaceful it all looked, how spacious and clean! The kitchen clock struck three. She always kept it five minutes fast—another of the good old habits they laughed at her about. Presently the other clocks of the neighbourhood began to chime, and then, so silent was the night, she heard through their interstices the solemn toll of Big Ben. Each stroke seemed to swell in her breast like an impersonal sorrow, round itself out, and die away.

Moving stiffly—for even in this brief pause her tired muscles had begun to set—she brought in the things from the passage. The room she had been looking at, the room in which the calm notes of Big Ben had resounded, disappeared under the familiar clutter and maladjustment of daily life. Oh yes, she was glad to leave it!

As she was going upstairs, the front door opened. Jennifer came in.

'Did you have a nice time, my pet? Was Ken there?'

'Good Lord, Mum, what on earth have you been doing

at this time of night? You'll never be down in the morning.'

'I'm just going to have a bit of a wash,' Florence answered evasively. 'I won't be long.'

'Be as long as you like, far as I'm concerned. I don't intend to wash an inch. I'm far too tired.'

'You ought to wash your feet, girl, whatever else you don't. A woman needs to wash her feet every night of her life. And if you don't get into the habit of it now——'

'I know, I know! I'll be sorry for it later.'

The bathroom was on the half landing. Of all the rooms in the house, it was the most squalidly congested; but Florence was there to clean herself, not it. Tapering the flow of water to a discreet trickle, she undressed and washed from head to foot—as thoroughly and expeditiously as she had cleaned the kitchen. Then, having put on her clothes again, she stole upstairs in the darkness, past Sheila and Tom, past Jasper and Peggy. The stairway to the attic was steep; she had to pause halfway up it to get her breath. As she stood there, it seemed as though the whole weight of the house dragged from her shoulders. Well, she would soon be rid of it—for now, just as in the kitchen's thorough turnout, she could see before her, plain and straightforward, what remained to be done. Poor Jerome! Little did he think that in getting his fine roomy house he was fastening this burden on her. But so it had to be. The bombs, falling everywhere else, had left it untouched. In the housing shortage after the war, she could not have refused to let Sheila and, after Sheila, Jasper, set up their married homes under its roof; and, once she had let them in, she could not turn them out. For a time, she had supposed that one or other of the young couples would move elsewhere, the more so when Sheila and Jasper began quarrelling. But their quarrels only rooted them, for each was determined to oust the other. The will she had made after Jerome's death settled the leasehold on the three children, and this they knew. Jennifer declared that she wouldn't take it as a gift, all she wanted was her share in cash; but the other two were bent on possession, and growled round each other like two dogs disputing a bone. They had been such loving children, too. Strange to remember it now!

Shrugging off these memories with a sigh, she climbed the remaining stairs, tiptoed past Mr. Laver's bedroom, and entered her own.

She could truly call it her own. No one came near it; it might have been in Timbuctoo. There was no reason to have hidden her preparations, but she had done so, and now she brought them out—the rolls of sticky tape, the placard, the moistened yellow soap for stopping the key-hole. The two attics had formerly been servants' bedrooms, and gas fires were fixed in front of their narrow grates. The flues went up the chimneys, the draughts rushed down, and while the rooms had been used for storing Jerome's odd-ments this harmed nobody. But after his death, when she was taking in lodgers for a livelihood, she had had surrounds put in; and knowing from Jerome what tricks some builders will be up to, she had stood by while the work was done to make sure there was no scamping. Her flue had rusted a little, the fit was no longer perfect, but she had puttied up the crannies a few days before, and sticky tape would make all sure. The window would be the worst job, for it was large, and the woodwork was weathered and shrivelled. So she would do that first.

To reach the upper part of the window, she mounted

on a chair. Suddenly it was borne in on her how conspicuous she must be, standing there with the curtains
drawn back, and crucified by the light behind her. The
street was empty, the houses opposite were dark. But how
was she to know that from those darkened house-fronts
eyes were not watching her, that windows would not be
thrown up, lights turned on, dozens of figures point and
gesticulate, dozens of voices shout out, 'Here, what's going
on?' 'What's she doing?' 'WHAT ARE YOU DOING, MRS.
CULLEN?' None of this happened, and after a while her fear
was forgotten in the difficulty of controlling sticky tape.
She felt no other fear. She knew what she was doing; she
had it all cut and dried. It was too real to be afraid of. It
was so real that once or twice the smell of the gas she would
presently turn on seemed to be already in her nostrils. Two
rounds of sticky tape made sure of the flue. The paste of
soap and water went so obligingly into the keyhole that it
was quite a pleasure—as if she were handling a good
dough. She rolled the blanket which was to lie along the
bottom of the door. She would tape the door, too, last of all,
but she felt there should also be a rolled-up blanket. One
can't be too careful, and in the suicides by gas one reads of
in the Sunday papers there is always a rolled-up blanket.
The feel of the blanket made her realize that she was
perished with cold. It was silly not to have lit the fire, so
as to warm up the room a bit, but now it was too late to be
worth it, she would slip on her dressing-gown instead. She
pulled forward the old easy chair to the hearth. There she
would sit, cosy and quiet in her dressing-gown, and breathing in the fumes that were so familiarly in her mind that
she kept on thinking she was already smelling them. She'd
be thankful to sit down.

But not yet; she must keep on her feet, for if she once sat down she might well doze straight off. She fetched the placard—she had made it from the lid of a white cardboard box, boring two holes in it and knotting in a bit of string, so that it could hang from the doorknob—and uncorked the bottle of ink. Leaning against the chest of drawers, she wrote in large capitals, which she thickened with additional strokes of the pen, 'CAUTION. GAS ESCAPING.' She carried it out on the landing. It dropped from her hand. Good Lord, there was an escape of gas! If anyone were to strike a match, the whole house might go up!

Knowing only that there was danger, and that people must be warned, she banged on Mr. Laver's door and ran downstairs. She was just about to rouse Peggy, when she noticed that the smell of gas was much fainter. The escape must be on the top floor. She ran back, stumbling on the hem of her dressing-gown. There was no doubt about the smell, and no doubt where it was coming from.

'Mr. Laver! Mr. Laver!'

He was snoring.

'*Mr. Laver!*'

She didn't dare make much noise. Sheila was only waiting for an excuse to get the poor fellow out, and this would supply it.

'Mr. Laver, it's me. And I'm coming in.'

Thank the Lord, the door wasn't locked. It yielded, a screw of newspaper dropped, an enveloping smell of gas rushed out, and immediately the door halted on some obstacle. The obstacle was a mackintosh. She could feel it with her fingers, but the aperture was not wide enough for her to get her hand in. Her Sunday umbrella was next door, and had a hooked handle. Poking and clawing with this, she managed to free the door sufficiently to put her hand in, switch on the light, and shove the mackintosh aside.

Turn off the tap, break a window-pane. Thanks to the Sunday papers, it was as plain as the Ten Commandments. But where was Mr. Laver? Instead of an armchair drawn up before the hearth, with Mr. Laver in it, there was only the folding table with two envelopes displayed, one addressed 'For the Coroner', the other 'Mrs. Florence Cullen'. Mr. Laver was in the last place she would have expected; he was in his bed. His eyes had turned up; he looked like a boiled fish. The right thing to do was to get him to the window, where he would breathe the fresh air. She took hold of his shoulders and tried to haul him up. His head rolled forward with a dreadful meekness, but she could not move him; it was beyond her strength. *Dash cold water on the face.* . . . She had read that somewhere or other; and before calling Tom and Jasper, and letting it all come out, she could try cold water. There was a tap and runaway on the landing, and this had been partitioned off and a washstand put there so that Mr. Laver could use it when he couldn't get into the bathroom. The ewer was empty. It took some time to fill, and when she came back the smell of gas had lessened, and Mr. Laver's legs were stirring under the quilt, as if he were trying to climb out of his unconsciousness by a ladder. She emptied the ewer over him. He shuddered, but that was all. She ran for more water, and this time when she returned his eyes were back in their place, and looked at her, and then looked away. He would get over it. Presently, she would go down and make him some tea. She could do with a cup herself, her mouth was dry and she had a splitting headache. She

pocketed the two envelopes, and went to stand in the air
that flowed through the broken pane. The window was at
the back, and looked out on the backs of the houses in
Opal Street. Here and there a light was on. She could
smell frying. Someone was endeavouring to start up a
lorry. It was as if time, which had stopped, were now
going again.

There was a stir behind her.

'Are you feeling better?'

'I'm going to be sick.'

Before she could find anything for him to be sick into,
he was vomiting all over the bedclothes.

When she had cleaned him up as best she could, and
assured him that a little bit of extra washing meant nothing
to her, and that he would soon be all right, she went down
to the kitchen to make tea. While she waited for the kettle
to boil, she read his letter to her:

DEAR MRS. CULLEN,

I must apologize for any inconvenience I may cause
you by taking this step. No doubt it will be a shock to
you—I have always hidden my feelings, being somewhat of a solitary. All I can now say is that the heart
knoweth its own bitterness. In the brown suitcase under
my bed you will find a bundle of papers. Please burn
them unread—my poor pipings. I see no future for
them, or for myself. Once more, my apologies.

Yours truly,

RONALD LAVER

How like a man, she thought, steeling her heart. How
exactly like a man—expecting you to burn a great wadge
of papers when he knows that every fire in the house is gas

or electric. Was she to go off and have a bonfire on Hampstead Heath? It would have been a different matter if the range were still in use. . . . She turned and looked at it, gleaming in its coal-black lustre, and at the dresser, with every piece of crockery washed and polished, at the scrubbed woodwork, and the shining taps, and the clean curtains she had hung in the window; and everything she saw seemed to be reproaching her for a treachery. She had failed them. She had defaulted on her act of farewell, and was still here. The kettle boiled and boiled away while she stood weeping for misery and mortification and defeat.

A WORK OF ART

Pʀɪᴠᴀᴛᴇ charity still persists in England though mostly it is practised in the disorderly, hole-and-corner style recommended by Jesus. Mrs. Bernstein was so far in step with the welfare state that she used a paid administrator, but she did so for reasons of her own. If you have to go about in a wheel-chair, she said, you can't see things for yourself. Moreover, a benefactress of immense weight carried by grunting porters up to attics or down to basements (and misery is seldom domiciled on ground-floor level) is bound to create remark, and bring every cheat, thief, cadger, and social worker, not to mention hosts of other unfortunates, to settle like blowflies on the benefited one. So she availed herself of Miss MacTavish, whose muscular legs and unobtrusive bearing could get her in anywhere. Miss MacTavish had already got herself into a perfectly satisfactory life of her own. She was an artist, and illustrated children's books for a living. It was in the intervals of drawing little girls with turned-up noses offering apples to horses with classical profiles that she went about Mrs. Bernstein's business.

Every three months or so, Mrs. Bernstein would engage Miss MacTavish in strategic conversation to see if any professional do-goodery had lodged itself in her administrator's outlook. The results were reassuringly negative. The outlook remained that of the artist; no tendency to confuse making people a trifle better off with making people better clouded Miss MacTavish's appraising eye.

It was above all betterment that Mrs. Bernstein wished to avoid. She had been bettered in her youth and was of the opinion that it would be quite as nauseous to be bettered in maturity or in old age. She was even suspicious of bodily betterment, since the body is the envelope of the soul and not always reliably impermeable. Instead of carrying bundles of blankets and parcels of nourishing food, Miss MacTavish carried pound notes, which are easier both to convey and to conceal. But as one must not muzzle the ox that treadeth out the corn, she was free to give advice—provided that the advice was drawn from her own experience and that the money was given first.

'My Uncle Heinrich,' said Mrs. Bernstein, 'did it the other way round. And so I was always being trapped into performing a pound's worth of behaviour and then getting two and sixpence. That's not fair dealing. And one must not do things for them. Even the rich don't trust even the experts who do things for them. For the poor it is impossible. It would crush all the spontaneity of their taking.'

'I wonder that you are prepared to trust me,' said Miss MacTavish.

'Well, yes. Perhaps you'll run off with it. So you wanted it. So that's all right.'

Discovering Mrs. Bernstein was an enlarging experience, just as beginning to paint in oils had been, and Fiona MacTavish blessed the day when she had run up to steady the chair which was about to topple sideways into the Serpentine—an act that had led to a conversation about the Loch Ness monster, the best way of cooking carp, and the first of many invitations to lunch.

For several years she acted as Mrs. Bernstein's emissary

without ever questioning the method laid down for her. This was not mere docility. It seemed to her that the method worked uncommonly well. She saw people looking pleased, and could quit them without any sense of having smudged their pleasure. She saw—which is perhaps rarer— people who regularly received money from her and who met her again without the least trace of fear or calculation. Naturally, she did not always see these wonders, but they occurred oftener than she could have expected. Now and then she gave advice, which was warmly reciprocated in valuable recommendations about health, canaries, geranium cuttings, cockroaches, and so on. And in the course of time she became increasingly attached to Mrs. Bernstein, who became increasingly fatter, uglier, richer, and more versed in the *affaire Port Royal*—this last on the ground that it brought her closer to Mme. de Sévigné. It was Mr. Herzen who drove Miss MacTavish to question the absolute inadmissibility of doing things for those you give money to.

Mr. Herzen was solitary, sickly, hypochrondriacal, sometimes charming, always shiftless, and never continuing in one stay. When traced to a new lodging, he would explain that he had not been able to pay the rent, or that he had merely forgotten to do so, with the result that he had been cruelly evicted. Quite often, this was not so at all. He had paid, he had gone—the landlady just couldn't account for it. Disappearing thus for months on end and when traced being sicklier, sadder, shabbier, and distinctly reproachful—since he insisted on thinking he had somehow displeased his kind friends and been cast off by them—Mr. Herzen drove Miss MacTavish to take a stand.

'I really cannot go on looking for Mr. Herzen any longer, Mrs. Bernstein.'

'Still lost, poor man?'

'No, no. I've hunted him down again. This time he's in Finsbury.'

'*Mais qu'avez-vous de mourir si souvent ?*' murmured Mrs. Bernstein.

'In the most frightful hole, with the most appalling landlady. And it seems to me that we—that you—will be compelled into doing something for him.'

'I don't approve of doing.'

'I know you don't. I don't like the idea of it myself. But there are times when there's nothing for it but desperate measures. Now, listen. This is what I suggest....'

*

In the end, she got her way. A small furnished flat was found, with a pleasant landlady. It was redecorated, and to the landlady it was explained that Miss MacTavish was Mr. Herzen's person of business, and that he would pay his rent through her. By thus representing him as someone rich and strange, she hoped to pass off his obvious poverty, settled incompetence, and vagaries of temper. She thought she had done pretty well, but Mrs. Bernstein continued to assert that doing didn't do. So convinced was she of this that, though she still paid his rent and his allowance, she ceased to inquire about him—as though she knew by some private information that he was dead, but respected the privacy.

Presently it appeared that Mr. Herzen shared Mrs. Bernstein's rejection of the Deed. The pleasant landlady, now looking slightly hangdog, said one day, 'You know, dear, you mustn't think I'm taking money under false colours. But that ten bob a week Mr. Herzen pays me over and above for cleaning his rooms and so on—well, I'm only too ready to do for him, but he won't hear of it And how he manages about the dust and the smuts and the carpet sweepings I'm sure I do not know, for he hasn't brought down as much as a teacupful to the dustbin in the yard. And sometimes it really worries me, quite apart from the furniture, for it's as plain as a pikestaff that he's the kind of gentleman who needs doing for.'

Miss MacTavish said that Mr. Herzen might be afraid of his papers being disarranged.

'Yes, ducks. I recollect you told me he was consecrated in his work and not to be disturbed. Though I don't know when he does it, really. He's always out. He's gone out now.'

The next time she called, Mr. Herzen was out. And the next. Or perhaps it was she who was out—locked out. She had a most distinct impression that on the other side of the door someone was listening. Two could play at that game. Thrusting away all consideration of what Mrs. Bernstein would think of such behaviour—besides, Mr. Herzen was already an exception—she dropped the envelope with the money in it through the letter slot, walked partway downstairs, continued to pat with her feet, and listened. She heard the envelope being torn open. She heard his cough, exasperated by suppression and now let out to do its worst. Knocking on the door, banging on it and shouting, she at last overthrew the silence that lay behind it like a great mattress propped up to intercept bullets.

'Oh, dear! It's Miss MacTavish. I was asleep. Ah, it would be so. The first sleep I have had for days and days. Unlucky, eh?'

The envelope on the floor, the notes sticking out of his pocket, were the only clean things in the room. Dust lay thick on the furniture, cobwebs trailed from the ceiling and latticed the grimy window. Dirty and unshaven, he stood at bay in his den.

'Isn't it terrible? Isn't it terrible? And I have been so ill, I am still so ill, I cannot sleep because of my cough, and whatever I eat, it comes up again, I am poisoned through and through. And the woman downstairs, she does nothing for me, nothing! She puts milk for her cat and forgets me. Not that I have anything against the poor cat, you understand. If I were not so ill I would move, for it is killing me here. All this dust is so bad for my cough.'

'It must be. Poor Mr. Herzen, no wonder you feel ill. Mrs. Bernstein will be sorry to hear all this.'

'No, no! Don't tell her. I do not like to be a trouble to my friends. I shall struggle through somehow. Or I shall not. Every herring must hang by his own tail, eh? I do not like to complain.'

'Do you know what I would advise you to do?'

He started, and glared at her.

'What you need is to have this place given a thorough cleaning. You'll never get well breathing up all this dust. And you're certainly not strong enough to tackle it yourself. What you must do is to go to one of those shops where they sell Hoovers and ask them to send a man to demonstrate it.'

His laugh, still a merry charming laugh under its grime of malevolence, rang out. 'That is what I call a genial idea. Then I tell him I'll think it over, eh? Perhaps it would be surer if I paid a first deposit?'

'I didn't.'

'What? You did this yourself? Splendid!'

For he was so abjectly undeserving, so unsuccourably an alien and a misfit, that she had to re-establish some sort of contact, grease the slide for Mrs. Bernstein's money to flow into that cold quicksand of a pocket. Loyalty to Mrs. Bernstein dictated that. If Mrs. Bernstein did not help him, no one else would, since no one could possibly better him. But as she went homeward to her tidy studio, her tidy modest industry, the illustrations for *Jennifer Sees It Through* on her desk and the blue abstract on her easel, she was so filled with discouragement that she seemed to herself to be going nowhere at all.

*

Locking the door and waiting to make sure that this time the cheating hag's ugly feet had carried her downstairs and away, Mr. Herzen savoured the moment when he would turn back to his dirt, his solitude, his paradise and great work of art. He turned. There it was, his own, and grimier and grander than ever before, having been acknowledged by her submission and astonishment. How she had stared, pretending not to stare! And she had not seen the whole. She had not seen his bedroom, the skylight opened to the sooty rain, the spatterings from medicine bottles soiling the walls, the morass of dirty socks left steeping in the wash-basin—a splendid passage, one of his best. She had not seen the kitchenette. But she had seen enough to know what he thought of the bright little reformatory they had designed for him—insulting his misery with light paint and flowery walls—and to know that he was not a man to swallow insults. From the first moment of waking in this bourgeois kennel he had realized what to do with it, he had foreseen the masterpiece that he and time would create between them, stroke by patient stroke. 'How do you like it?' the woman had asked, bringing him his money. And he had replied that every day he liked it better. For even then, though she was blind to it, the masterpiece was taking form and the first cobwebs were mustering in the corners. Slow to get under way, tantalizingly slow and fitful, the process of deterioration had gathered impetus, sweeping him along with it, inspiring him to spill and scorch and knock over, so that whatever he did prompted a new invention of filth and squalor. And then, impalpable as a vapour, the quality of perfection had emerged, grave and austere, wrapping his inventions and contrivances and laboured-at dinginess in a solemn veil of inhumanity. Now when he went out, it was not to escape from the dis-commodities of creation, the dust that choked him, the fœtor that sickened him, but in order to return like a priest returning to the shrine, like a ghoul entering the rich charnel house and musingly rubbing its palms together as it looks round. Absorbed in his task, he had forgotten the motive that dictated it, the piece of grit round which this black pearl had accumulated.

Though the woman's intrusion had brought him that confirming satisfaction, she was superfluous; he did not require the assent of her dismay. Perfection and the Whole had come before her. He would not open the door again.

But the envelope must be attended to. It lay on the floor, pert, crisp and alien. He set his heel on it, grinding it to and fro on the dirty carpet. A cloud of dust flew up. When he lifted his heel and looked at the envelope, it had learned its place. It subserved a work of art.